Falcon

amara lynn

To those who fight for love.

Acknowledgments

As always, for Emma, for being my muse and writing partner in crime. Without you, these characters wouldn't exist for my mind to run away with. Lurve forever!

To Bird, I'm so glad I found you, somehow. Thank you for helping me make my birds the best they can be.

And to my queer writing community, thank you all for your support!

"As confident as is the falcon's flight

Against a bird, do I with Mowbray fight."

Richard II, act 1, scene 3

William Shakespeare

CHAPTER ONE

WHEN FORCED TO make a choice between themselves and others, people will *always* choose to save themselves, because people are all inherently flawed, selfish beings.

At least, that was what I used to think. Then I met Chayton. Pure, kind hearted, selfless Chayton. Together, we were a beautiful, chaotic disaster. Chay was selfish, at least when it came to me. But not in the same way as a normal person. Even in those selfish moments, he still somehow managed to be so damn selfless that it stabbed at my heart.

He wanted to save me when I was on the path of villainy as Raven—selfless. He let how he felt about me as Avari affect his judgment, and had been willing to let a *criminal* go free because of those feelings—selfish. He wanted to make me happy—selfless. He almost got himself killed by demons chasing after me—selfish. Completely and utterly selfish. And damn it, so was I when it came to him. I tried to be selfless, tried to leave because I wanted to protect him, as my dad had my mother before me, and where had that gotten us? Nowhere, except in the middle of the Muir Woods with Chayton bleeding out in my arms and nearly dying—which he would have, if not for my father's divine intervention. That really was a miracle, performed right before my eyes.

After that, I couldn't be selfless. When it came to Chayton, I wanted to be selfish. I wanted him, regardless of the consequences, regardless of if we were actually terrible for each other. Chay really was so damn stubborn. But I was glad for it. I wanted him to be selfish when it came to me, too.

Every day since then, that moment had haunted me. That look of terror in his eyes filled my dreams, the horror repeating over and over in my head. Each time I saw his face, the flames of the hellish moment reignited anew and set my heart alight.

"Avaaa! Houston to Ava, do you read?" Kaiden's voice brought me back to the present.

City noises returned to my ears—cars and people and the breeze, still a bit chilly this time of year. We were almost to the Asian Ghetto now. I'd spaced out most of our walk there. Kaiden had ambushed me after class, as usual.

"Huh?" I swatted his hand away as he waved it in front of my face.

"I said, you never told me what you and Chayton did for Valentine's day!" Kaiden waggled his eyebrows at me.

"None of your business, that's what," I mumbled and looked away.

"Aw come on, I want juicy deets! It was his birthday, too, right? Did you guys do it? Did you give him a little favor? Dish!"

2

Kaiden, for all his annoyance and hyperness and loquaciousness, was actually a good, true friend. When I needed someone to have my back, he was there. Literally, and with knives, which was equal parts relieving and alarming. We shared a bond, in our otherness, our rebellion, our refusal to meet the status quo. Somehow, I had actually made another friend. The first had been Chay, who was now my friend, and had been my rival and almost enemy for a time, and then my everything. Chay had saved me from myself, from my loneliness. And I almost left that behind. Damn it, I was thinking about it *again*. The ghosts of that day haunted my every thought. Like a demon on my trail, it always seemed to know where I was and came for me.

"Well?"

Ugh, he was so hung up on sex shit. I didn't get what the big deal was with people and sex. Was that something people normally thought about so much?

"Shut it," I said, and stomped ahead of him on the sidewalk.

In truth, we hadn't managed to get much of anywhere on Valentine's day, and it was kind of a shitty day. We went out to our favorite Mexican place, we went back to my room, to be alone, and I was nervous as hell because, damn it I always was with him, and I was dealing with the shock of almost losing him still. That, and it was *Chayton*, and about everything he did or said just cut me to the quick, left me reeling and drowning and sinking.

Things had started to heat up, but then I accidentally elbowed my remote and turned the TV on. There was a huge heist on the news, and he got that look in his eyes, the one that said "I need to go help."

Even though I argued that he didn't, that this was why we had law enforcement, he'd gone. That was the first time I

3

couldn't bear to watch the news, waiting for him in silence and misery to return to me.

And I waited all night, and all I got was a text saying he was back safe and goodnight.

That had been a few weeks ago, and we'd fought hard about that one, which I still regretted. Our silences had never been too awkward, but now they were awkward and heavy with unspoken words. I wondered if it was just me being paranoid.

"What is up with you lately?" Kaiden stepped in front of me again, his hands on his hips and a pouty scowl on his face. "You keep spacing out."

"It's nothing." We were almost to the Asian Ghetto, thank God. I stepped around him and hurried the rest of the way.

I opted for ramen today, while Kaiden skipped over to Gyro's.

"Why don't you want to do anything fun anymore? We were having so much fun before, and now I can't even get you to take me for a fly!" Kaiden said as we were starting our walk back to campus.

"Shh! We're right out in the open." I stopped in my tracks and looked around. Ahead of us, a couple of girls giggled, off in their own college drama world I supposed. Wouldn't that be nice, to be normal and ignorant? I let out a sigh of relief. Kaiden and his big mouth.

"Oops! Sorry!" He gave me a sheepish grin.

"You need to calm down. We're in public."

Kaiden frowned and pouted his lip at me. "I'm sorry."

"One of these days, you'll be the death of me."

"Aw, you really think that?"

"It's a damn good possibility. You never shut the hell up, and you're way too hyper for your own damn good. You're just so...extra."

"Oh, come on! Don't you think I'm endearing?" He leaned closer, the mischievous gleam in his eye. "I'm the guacamole to your burrito!"

I scoffed. Did I find it endearing? "You're ridiculous."

"I'm entertaining! Stop being such a mean friend!"

"If you wanted a nice friend, you would have chosen someone else."

"Good point! What I really wanted was a badass fire flinging nephil—"

"Shh!" We were almost back to campus, where it was more crowded, and more likely someone might hear. He laughed and danced out of my reach, his smile showing he had done that one on purpose.

I huffed and blew my messy black bangs out of my eyes. "What does that mean?" I asked.

"What?"

"The guacamole to my burrito?"

Kaiden snickered. "Cuz that shit's extra!"

Ha, okay. I'd give him that one.

Kaiden was a thorn in my side, but he kept me on my toes. He was someone who knew my secrets, really knew me, and accepted me for me.

I could've done without how damn talkative he was. I wondered if he only hassled me because he thought it was amusing to get a rise out of me. Or maybe, he was trying to get some fireworks out of me. After all, when I was angry, you'd better watch out, or you might catch fire. When things caught fire, people noticed, and would come for miles just to watch them burn. I had learned that all too well during my escapades as Raven. A few explosions was all it took to get on the news. I missed that feeling. I couldn't do that anymore. For several reasons.

Kaiden was snickering again.

"You big mouth," I mumbled and gave him a nasty glare. I elbowed him.

"Ouch!" He said, in obvious mock pain. When he'd recovered, he bumped shoulders with me. I bumped his back fondly. "I think it's hilarious how touchy you are. Or maybe I should say prickly? You're like a cute little cactus!"

"I think it's been well established that I'm not a nice person. And I'm not cute." I trudged onward, across the campus, past the Campanile that always cut through the sky.

"Bah, that's not true. You're not as mean as you think you are."

I narrowed my eyes at him. "What makes you think that?"

"We have fun together, don't we? I've seen you smile and laugh around me. That, and I see the way you look at Chayton. You lovebirds!" He clutched his hands together and made some goo goo eyes at me.

I sighed and opened the door to my housing building. He had no clue how apt that description was. But he could never learn the truth. I could only imagine the field day Kaiden would have with that one. I saw what he did to those images of Falcon on his wall of newspaper clippings. What did his roommate think of his little collection? I doubted it changed their opinion *too* much. I mean, Kaiden was *so* much to deal with already. His roommate probably just tried to keep to themself and didn't pay much mind to the out of control mess on Kaiden's side of the room.

"Pff. Whatever." I headed to my room, Kaiden trailing behind me. Whether I liked it or not, he was right. I was a sourpuss who hated everyone, and I was on a bad streak there for a while, which might've turned much worse if not for Chay. Despite it all, though, I had a soft side. An intimate side. Chay had seen it, and Kaiden had seen it in small doses.

I hated how well he understood me. And that's why, beneath it all, I considered Kaiden a true friend.

CHAPTER TWO

CHAYTON

I WAS FLYING through the skies, frantic, stomach in knots. It felt like there were a thousand voices in my head, all screaming contradictory things.

"He's no good for you," my brain said. "It's not meant to be. Just let him leave."

"Don't let him go. He needs you, and you need him. You love him, don't you? Then fight for him! Don't let go!" My heart cried out, louder than my brain.

My heart was winning the war raging in my head, and my wings carried me, swift and true to my heart's desire.

And then, chaos struck, right through my chest like a stake through the heart. Every day I put my life on the line as Falcon, and yet, I'd never once considered my life to be at risk like it was in that moment when Ava was holding me and I was bleeding out in his arms.

"Chayton! Chay!" Ava's voice cried out, muffled by my thumping heart as panic set in. I was going to die. All because I couldn't bear to live without him.

Then the blood burst forth, slow at first, a deadly red flower blossoming on my chest. I would never forget the look of terror in Ava's eyes.

I woke up.

My back was sticky with sweat and I was panting for air. I untangled myself from my damp comforter, which I'd gotten wrapped up in like a burrito during my night of tossing and turning, dreaming and remembering things I wanted desperately to forget.

The first rays of daylight were peaking through the blinds. I picked up my phone from my nightstand to check the time. Not quite five A.M. I sighed. There was a text from my cousin, Dy, too. He asked if everything was okay, because it'd been awhile since I checked in with him. I had never continued our last check in conversation, and had left the one before that on read, too. I was probably making him worry.

My responses had been a bit sparse since I became involved with Ava. Who I still hadn't told him about. I wasn't afraid because he was a guy, though. Dy knew I was gay. I'd had a few crushes on guys growing up, but nothing that ever developed into something other than friendship before Ava.

No, it wasn't my queerness. It was…Ava. I wasn't sure what he'd think of Ava, and I was scared.

I texted him a quick reply: *Sorry, Dy. Been busy with midterms. Call you later?*

It wasn't a lie, but it wasn't the complete truth, either. I didn't expect an answer yet; it was central time back home.

Across the room, my roommate, Jossia, was still asleep. He wasn't a light sleeper, something I was thankful for. I was also thankful Ava didn't share the same dorm room as me. The last thing I wanted was to be a burden to him. Was it already too late for that? At least he didn't have to know about my nightmares. Not yet.

When was the last time I had night terrors? Long enough that I had trouble remembering. Before coming to Berkeley, shortly after starting high school. And yet, here they were again, out of nowhere like the demon that had almost taken my life.

Chala used to tell me that dreams were a window into the soul. That our subconscious mind perceived things our conscious mind could not, and to heed warnings given during dreams.

"What if all my dreams are nightmares?" I'd asked her.

"Then you should take extra caution, my little falcon, so your nightmares don't come true."

What if they already had? First my parents, and then Chala, and then… Ava. Almost twice now.

Not for the first time, I wished Chala were here to comfort me, to pull me into her arms and tell me everything would be okay as many times as it took for me to believe it. When she said it, it seemed to work. When Dy said it, it seemed to work. But when I did, it didn't. I clutched my knees up to my chest and heaved. Tears slid down my cheeks, surprising me. It'd been a long time since I wept for Chala. After she passed, I tried to tell myself it would be okay. Every day, every hour, every second. I tried to carry on, and slowly, my life mended back together, though it wasn't without extreme effort.

I mourned her long after it was appropriate to. If not for

Dy's support, I might've kept spiraling in my depression.

Then I met Ava.

When I saw him for the first time, before I even talked to him, there was something about him that drew me in. I never told him this, but I noticed him before we ever got paired up in our chemistry lab. His presence was magnetic to me, yet his glare was so intense it made me hesitate to talk to him.

We clashed, we fought, we collided. Then we fell in love. It hadn't been easy. It'd been a rough couple months.

We were an unlikely pair. Against the odds, we'd met, in this big world, in this sprawling city, which according to Ava, was infested with demons.

I couldn't see them. I didn't have to, though. One had impaled me right through the chest.

Now, those terrible moments where I almost bled out in Ava's arms kept haunting me in my dreams in place of the ones I used to have of losing those around me I loved. I still remembered thinking at least I'd die in the arms of the one I loved. I'd die fighting for what my heart wanted.

Then, a miracle happened, and I lived.

I was alive. I was still here. And, most importantly, Ava stayed. I hadn't lost him. He hadn't lost me.

Everything was okay. Everything was okay.

I slipped out of bed, quietly, though I probably wouldn't wake the soundly sleeping, worry free Jossia from his peaceful slumber, which was probably full of good dreams or a void of nothingness. What I wouldn't give for a night devoid of nightmares again.

In the shower room, I undid my ponytail and combed through my hair, which was in frizzy waves from being in a braid, before getting under the steaming hot water and basking in the warmth. These days, I lost track of time and stood in the scalding water, breathing slowly in and out as everything sank in anew for the day. When I started the year, I always woke up with a smile on my face, ready to face the day. I didn't zone out and take too long in the shower. I didn't forget my clothes or to brush my teeth or braid my hair, or remember that I hadn't even done last week's assignments.

I didn't do those things. I was the ideal student, always prepared, well kept, and had everything together.

I didn't *used* to do those things. Not for a long time now. I was better. I wasn't a mess anymore.

And just like that, I was in a panic again, right in the middle of the shower.

Deep breaths, deep breaths. In and out.

It felt like I was stabbed all over again, a phantom ache of that moment which kept repeating itself in my waking and sleeping hours. I touched my chest. There wasn't even a scar there. Physically, it was like it never even happened. In my mind though, it had left a fresh wound that tore open my past scars anew.

I leaned my head against the shower wall and kept my eyes shut tight until I calmed down. When I stepped out of the shower, the whole room was filled with a thick steam from me having the hot water turned so high.

Another person came in while I was combing my hair and said "What the hell, man?"

"Sorry," I offered, making no attempt to explain myself because anything I came up with would just be a lie, and I couldn't bring myself to fib. I hurried out once I finished dressing, pulling my hair into a ponytail instead of braiding it as I walked back to my room.

I schlepped my way to class, and spaced for half of it, taking just enough notes to get by. I could always look at the lecture notes online later, thankfully. I'd been doing that a lot more lately. It didn't used to be this hard to concentrate.

Ava had a long class today, and Kaiden would probably bug him for lunch afterward, so I went off wandering on my own. Normally, I would take my Falcon outfit with me. Today, I passed, and instead went out in my street clothes — a knitted poncho, jeans, hemp shoes, and a blue t-shirt that said Berkeley on it that'd been a present from Dy when I got my acceptance letter.

It was the end of February, so it was still chilly. I was glad I didn't have to remove my clothes like Ava did to bring out my wings. I just touched my earring as soon as I was alone, and I was good to go.

I flew up to a rooftop and perched there. That's all I did, just perched. Sat. Thought.

The buzz of the city filled my ears, the people below going on with their lives. They would go about their day, regardless of what happened, regardless of if Falcon existed. More often than not, all I did was fly up to a high spot and space out. Falcon wasn't needed as much as superheroes always were in comics and movies.

Sometimes, in the middle of the night when I couldn't sleep, I'd fly to the top of the Campanile on campus. It was eerily quiet there at night, unlike other places in the greater Bay area, some of which never seemed to sleep. Other times, I needed the noise, the horns and engines and people. All of it reminded me to focus on the present and stop thinking about the past.

Nothing good lurked in the shadows of my past. Being alone and in complete silence was becoming less and less appealing each day.

*Everything will be okay. Everything **is** okay.*

I'd started repeating that again more and more, just like

I had after Chala was gone, since Dy wasn't here to say it to me. It never helped. Maybe if I didn't give up, it would.

I wanted comfort. I wanted closeness. I wanted Ava.

I headed back to campus around the time I thought Ava would be getting back to his room. Sure enough, we arrived about the same time. An uppity Kaiden was following him, both of them holding containers of food.

Ava's gaze landed on me, and his face changed from his cool, even, done with everyone and everything glare to the look that was only for me. It was intense, longing, protective, and above all else, affectionate. Loving.

"Hey, Chay." He smiled at me. It made my heart flutter. When I first came around, he never smiled. Now he did every time he saw me.

"Hey, Ava."

"Yo, Chayton!" Kaiden chimed in.

"Hey," I said, nodding to Kaiden and keeping my face neutral.

"Later, Kaiden." Ava waved a hand at Kaiden without looking at him.

"Aw, you don't wanna eat together?"

"Nope," Ava said without hesitation.

"Fiiiine. I see how it is. You want alone time with your squish." Kaiden snickered and skipped off.

In some ways, I still thought Kaiden was a bad influence on Ava. He was also a loud mouth, and part of me was afraid he would blab all Ava's secrets at any moment, though unintentionally. At least he didn't know that I was Falcon, which was definitely for the best.

Ava sighed and shook his head. "Coming to my room?"

"Yeah." I smiled and took his hand, leaning against him the rest of the way to his door.

Kaiden knew all Ava's secrets, same as me. For a bit

there, he knew more than me even, which hurt. Even though I understood it hadn't all been Ava's doing, he entrusted Kaiden with information about his father and went out stirring up trouble to find him—with Kaiden along—all of which he kept me completely in the dark about.

Ava let us in and sat on his bed, dropping his bag carelessly on the floor and popping open his food container. He didn't turn on the TV, though less than a month ago he would've.

I didn't watch the news much either these days. I didn't have to worry about seeing Raven on the news anymore. When I spotted him on TV recently, I was shocked and hurt, and practically in tears when I confronted him about it. When I saw how remorseful Ava looked about the whole thing, I couldn't find it in myself to stay mad. The Ava from when we first met wouldn't think twice about setting a thing or two on fire, and might've ended up doing much worse if not for me. Ava wasn't the same as when we met. I hoped I was rubbing off on him, that he really had taken my words to heart, and that he didn't want to be Raven anymore.

Ava was staying safe now. He told me he had to keep a low profile because the demons could still be in the area, and that his dad had to lure them away. He didn't even want to risk going out for a fly with me or Kaiden, and especially not by himself.

I was secretly glad, because it meant there wouldn't be any more accidental Raven fiascos again. The most recent ones had put Falcon under fire, and with me making appearances less and less, people were talking even more. The tabloids were eating it up. I hoped they would let it die, soon.

"You want some?" Ava asked, holding up a fork full of noodles.

"No, I'm good." I should have eaten something, but lacked an appetite lately. I didn't want to take any of Ava's food, though it was sweet of him to offer.

I leaned against him while he ate. Perhaps too often, all I did was stare at him, afraid he could vanish at any moment, just like my parents and Chala. I didn't want to be alone. The scars opened further, the ache in my heart grew.

"What?" He raised a brow at me, giving me a confused look.

Every moment, I was afraid Ava would leave again. Every moment, I was afraid it would all come crashing down.

Ava would change his mind, decide it was too dangerous to stay, and he'd be gone. My heart wouldn't be able to take it.

"Nothing," I said, and just smiled, as I always did, like nothing was wrong, like I wasn't falling apart on the inside.

But I was.

CHAPTER THREE

AVARI

EVERY TIME CHAY was out there, as Falcon, I was so worried that I couldn't concentrate on anything. And yet, as worried as I was, as curious as I was, I didn't turn on the news. I was too scared. I couldn't bear the thought of him out there, flying around, fighting, or worse, getting hurt.

I didn't think the demons would attack him again. I was pretty sure they'd only attacked him because he'd been in the way of me. Still, fear clung at me like a wraith, persistently whispering in my ear that Chay was in danger, that Chay would be hurt.

Every time I thought of him out there, it was accompanied by that moment again, a bloodied horn through his chest.

"Ava!" *Knock knock knock.* "Ava!" *Knock knock knock.* "Avari!" *Knock knock knock.*

Kaiden pounded on my door, and it was way too early. I groaned as I was forced back into the present. That was probably for the best, given my train of thought.

"Aaaavaaaaa." *Knock. Knock knock.*

"I'm coming!" I sighed and pulled myself out of bed, stretching briefly before yanking the door open. Kaiden usually came around, often too early for my liking, wanting to go to breakfast together before classes. I'd much rather it be Chay, but this was my lot in life—the annoying sidekick. "What do you want?" I asked, even though I was well aware of what he wanted.

"Let's go get breakfast! Did I wake you up?"

"No, I was up." I rolled my eyes and smoothed my unkempt hair and my sleep wrinkled t-shirt while stuffing my feet into my boots.

"Then let's go! Hurry!"

"I'm coming, I'm coming," I said, grabbing my black button up shirt and my wallet from my desk.

We walked along the campus, which was just waking up for the morning, only a few students here and there, many in pajamas at this hour. The joys of being in college— people could (and would) show up to classes in their pajamas, which I thought was trashy, but I guessed that was just me.

We veered off campus territory and headed towards Little Gem, my favorite waffle place.

Kaiden danced around into my field of view to walk backwards in front of me. "Hey, why don't we go out on the town soon? I miss flying!"

"Shh!" I glared at the use of the word flying, even though it was early and there were few people about. "I already told you no before. I can't go out."

"But—"

"But nothing. Drop it." I gave him my best pissed off Raven glare and hoped I could be even one iota as intimidating as Chayton's Falcon glare. It was amazing how he could glare like that, yet could also look so damn sweet.

"Awww. But this is so boring! We never do anything interesting anymore!"

"Welcome to college life. It should be boring and dull, and full of studying. Why don't you try that?"

"Pff! Who needs to study?"

I rolled my eyes. "Probably you, based on that comment. What's your major again?"

"Art!" Kaiden grinned and flashed his hands up at me. Ah, right. I remembered now, the paint under his fingernails that time he patched me up from our first run in with a demon.

"That makes sense."

Kaiden laughed. "You think it suits me?"

"Yeah. Now I understand why you're all over the place. You're one of those secretly genius artist types," I said, half facetious. Outrageous abstract artist seemed perfect for Kaiden. I'd bet his art was as wild and bright as him.

"Ah! I'm glad you think so!" Kaiden stared at me with those star struck eyes, and I rolled mine again at him.

"Whatever." It wasn't really a compliment, but it was so like Kaiden to take it as one.

"We should go somewhere for spring break!" Kaiden and I took our seats and started eating, him talking with his mouth full.

"I plan on spending spring break with Chay and holed up in my room."

"What?" Kaiden gave me his puppy dog eyes. "But that's

so boring!"

I rolled my eyes at him. I wanted my peace and quiet. I wanted time alone with Chay, and between Kaiden's pestering, classes, and Chay's superhero stuff, we hardly ever got a moment for only us. I was feeling way too pent up because of it.

"Don't you wanna go to the beach with me?" He continued when I didn't say anything. "There'll be lots of cuties in swimsuits!"

I raised a brow. "Why do I care about that?"

"I mean, I know you're taken, but you can look and not touch!" Kaiden waggled his eyebrows at me.

"Look and not touch?" I narrowed my eyes at him. What the hell did that mean? I didn't understand how regular people who were not anti-social edgelords operated.

"You know, check people out? Scope out hotties?"

I continued to stare at him in a mix of disgust and confusion. "I don't get it."

"I'm always on the lookout. If someone looks attractive to me, I check 'em out a bit! If I get a vibe off 'em or they check me out, too, I move in for flirtation!"

If someone looked attractive? I hadn't ever done anything like that. His words were lost on me.

"I still don't get it."

"When you're just walking down the street, you don't ever see someone you think is hot? Sexy?" He swayed his fork across my face, as if to illustrate a person walking, his eyes trailing after the untensil.

"No?"

Kaiden had leaned too close yet again, something he always did when he was worked up or excited. I leaned away.

"What about Chayton? You didn't see him and think

'damn he's hot' when you met?"

"No. He was just another person. I never thought about it."

"Then how did you know you even liked him?" Kaiden was in full interrogation mode, and I wasn't in the mood (was I ever?). Answering his questions as quickly as possible was probably the easiest way to get him off the subject, though, so whatever.

"After spending time with him and getting to know him, I started to connect with him."

"Oh! I know! I bet you're demisexual!"

"What is that?"

"It means you don't feel sexual attraction for someone without a deep emotional connection."

Could that be it? I always thought I just didn't have an interest in people, period. As much as I avoided people, and so, lacked friends, I never had anyone to talk to about things like this. Kaiden had actually brought up a good point. Imagine that.

"And there Rocket Man goes again, off in space." Kaiden chuckled beside me.

"Oh, shut it. I was thinking about what you said."

"And?"

I shrugged. "I dunno. Maybe you're right."

"Yeah?" Kaiden grinned. "So, ya know... Have we connected?" He wiggled his eyebrows suggestively.

I rolled my eyes at him. "Pff. I'll stick with Chay, thanks."

Kaiden sighed. "I guess I'll drop the sex talk for now. Look, there is something actually important I wanted to tell you."

"What's that?" I raised a brow. Kaiden looked way too serious to be pulling my leg.

"They're still out there, you know." Kaiden leaned closer and whispered, showing discretion for once in his life. "The demons."

I leaned back to put distance between us. "I know that."

"Then why aren't you doing anything about it?"

"My dad will handle it. If I intervene, I'll just keep drawing more to the area. I have to lay low."

Kaiden frowned and planted his hands on the table. "Ava, you can't run from this. It's like, your density!"

"What?"

"Have you not seen Back to the Future, man? Oh, well, nevermind. It's your destiny, you know?"

"Shut up."

"But there's like, a ton. You don't understand. We've gotta do something!"

I slammed my hands on the table and stood up. A couple people turned their heads, and I sank back down quickly and leaned in close to him. "No, you don't understand. My dad will handle it. We aren't doing anything about it. Got it?"

Kaiden looked disappointed, but he nodded in assent. "Fine, fine. I got it. We aren't doing anything."

"Good. Now drop it." I dug back into my waffles before they got too cold. I really hoped I made my point, and Kaiden would stop pestering me about it. Now if only he'd stop pestering me all together, that'd be nice. Pff, as if.

CHAYTON

I SAT ATOP a high building and gazed out over the booming Bay city. I watched below, while the ordinary people carried on with their ordinary lives.

Had I ever been so ordinary, so carefree? Once, maybe. I couldn't remember now.

The city wasn't loud enough to drown out my thoughts, my fears, my worries. I glided to a lower building to better hear the cars and horns and people.

I ran my gloved hands over my head and took a couple deep breaths as I tried to quiet my loud mind. Ava didn't know this, but I was going out as Falcon a lot less than he thought since my brush with death. I rarely acted, even if I was in uniform.

In fact, I'd begun to wonder why I ever thought this was a good idea. I had happened upon my abilities, and this particular use for them, all on accident. What if this whole thing had been just that? An accident? I had already inadvertently had a hand in creating one villain rival in Raven, Ava's supervillain persona born from his frustration with my friendly demeanor, and only further fueled by our similarities. How long before I unwillingly drew more villains to me, to hurt people, destroy, and pose bigger threats than a mere robber?

I wasn't sure I could do this anymore. I wasn't sure I wanted to. It used to help me, by keeping me occupied, and now, nothing seemed to keep the demons of my thoughts away.

A siren pulled me out of my thoughts and back to the present. I glided from building to building, following the sirens, eventually taking off into the sky to keep up. It was a welcome distraction from my wild mind. I wouldn't interfere unless I thought the emergency responders couldn't handle it themselves.

I flew ahead of the police cars in an attempt to scope out things. Someone dressed in bright orange, hood pulled up, ran out of a convenience store, making a sharp turn down an alleyway before the cops would likely see. The sirens wailed louder, and the police car screeched to a stop in front of the store. Two officers got out of the vehicle.

Instead of going after the perpetrator, they'd go into the store and interview the clerk, probably asking for video evidence, and after reviewing that, put it on the news and put out a warrant. All while the person was still within the vicinity of the crime scene, getting away. They were only following their protocols. But I didn't have that problem. Falcon could catch up to the perp in no time and have them back to the police before they were finished interviewing the store's staff.

I took off in the direction the person had run, scanning the sidewalks and backstreets for the person in orange. That was an odd color for a convenience store hold up. A brief hint of familiarity prickled at the back of my mind at that particular shade of orange. I'd hold my theories for now, though.

The bright orange hoodie came into view. The hood had fallen down, revealing an uneven cropped mop of brown hair. My suspicions were only growing. I swooped down in the alleyway, cutting off the person. A red mask trimmed in gold framed bright, mischievous, blue eyes that I recognized instantly.

Kaiden. Slash. So it was him.

"Oh shit! F-F-Falcon?!" Slash about faced and tried to take off, a useless effort. I grabbed his hood.

"Stop right there!"

"Ack! No! Please, I didn't do anything wrong, I swear!" He put his hands on his head protectively. I hesitated, but kept my grip on his hood.

"I saw you run out of the convenience store."

"It's not what you think."

He didn't know I was Falcon, and that I knew he was Kaiden. He didn't know I knew about the demons. Falcon wouldn't think Slash had just escaped a run-in with demons, he'd think Slash was slashing up a store for kicks, living up to his namesake.

"What exactly is it then?" I asked, even though I wouldn't get the true answer.

"You wouldn't believe me." Slash's shoulders slumped. I almost loosened my grasp. Almost.

If I said anything else, I risked revealing myself.

I let go of his hood.

"Get out of here."

Slash stumbled forward and turned around to look at me with wide eyes. "Wait...What? Seriously? You're letting me go?"

I nodded. "You said you didn't do anything wrong. If that's true, I have no reason to turn you in. Just...try not to draw attention next time you're doing...whatever it is you were doing."

"Dude! Maybe you're not so bad after all!" Slash clasped his hands together and stared at me with bright eyes.

He really was something.

"Try to behave from now on," I said as I extended my wings to take off.

"I'll try, but no promises!" Slash grinned, while I grimaced at his reply. He saluted me as I flew off.

What was I going to do with him? If he was out there causing trouble like this, how could I ignore it? Though I wasn't bound by the same restrictions as an officer of the law, I did have a civil duty, as a protector. People expected me to do the right thing.

The problem was, I wasn't sure what the right thing was myself.

AVARI

AFTER MY CLASSES that day, I was surprised to find Chay waiting outside my room for me. This was usually his study and Falcon day, so I'd be lucky to get a couple texts.

"Hey. What's up?"

"Hey." We walked into my room together. "I need to show you something I found."

"What is it?"

He pressed a couple times on his phone and then held it up for me to read a news article.

There was a picture at the top, of a person in a convenience store, with two knives drawn. Not just your garden variety pocket knives, but like, fancy, engraved, hunting knives. Okay, one was practically a dagger.

A dagger I recognized.

My stomach dropped. I didn't have to read the article to surmise what it was about, but I did anyways.

A masked man held up a convenience store this morning at knife point. The man threw several knives at objects throughout the store, damaging goods and equipment, then rushed out of the store afterward.

The store owner stated the man did not ask for money or steal anything.

The man retrieved his knives after the act of vandalization, and according to the store owner, yelled "Sorry, dude!" before he ran out of the store.

"He was wearing one of those masks, like you see around Mardi Gras," the owner stated.

People are urged to contact the police with any information about this vandal.

God damn it, Kaiden.

I exhaled. "Damn him."

"There's a video. Want to see?" Chay scrolled down to the bottom and pointed to the clip.

I pressed play.

Kaiden spun around the store, three demons around him, though I doubted that a normal person would see that, if they watched the footage. He slashed his dagger through one and impaled another through the eye with his hunting knife. People in the store scurried to get out of the way when blades swooshed past their heads and impacted demons.

By the time all the demons were disposed of, the store was a wreck. Boxes were slashed open, liquids leaked all over the floor. A freezer door was shattered, glass bits scattered on the ground. The store clerk had their hands up, shaking as they stood there, eyes squeezed closed.

Kaiden grinned sheepishly, said something (the "Sorry dude!" I assumed), and then ran out of the store.

"What the hell, Kaiden?"

Chay turned his phone off and stuffed it back in his pocket. "What was he doing? Was he...fighting them?"

Them. The demons. I nodded. "Yeah."

What the hell was Kaiden thinking, going off on his own to deal with demons? He wasn't invincible. He was just a normal human with knives. Sure, he might have some demon blood in his veins, but he was still just a mortal, same as Chay, and as far as I was aware, myself. Having diluted demon blood didn't give him any physical advantage over the demons. The only thing it did was make it so he could see them and they left him alone. Unless he picked a fight with them, that is.

"Why is he doing this?"

"I don't know. I literally just talked to him this morning and told him to stay away from them. My dad's supposed to be luring them out of the area. Kaiden said there's still a lot around.."

Chay frowned. "Maybe you need to talk to him again. I —Falcon—can't let it go forever."

"I thought I'd gotten through to him. I don't know what he's thinking."

"I know he's probably just trying to help, but he needs to understand... That's not what it looks like to people."

"I know."

"I just want you to be safe. Whatever it takes." He took my hands in his and squeezed.

"I am being safe. It's Kaiden's delinquent, disobeying ass we've got to worry about."

I sat on my bed and let out a heavy breath.

"I know." Chay sat beside me, keeping hold of one of my hands. "You're sure he understood when you talked?"

"Yeah. He even repeated back to me 'we aren't doing anything'."

We exchanged a look of realization. *We.* Of course there was no we if it was just a *he.*

"Damn it, Kaiden!"

Chay squeezed my hand. "Talk to him again, okay? Just make sure he understands that him intervening hurts us. Er, well, you. You know."

"I know. He doesn't know about you being Falcon. I

promise."

He smiled and kissed my cheek. "I trust you with that."

"Just with that?" I raised my eyebrow at him. He looked away, but not before the look of guilt shot across his face.

"Chay? You don't trust me?"

"Ava... It's not that, it's just..." Chay sighed and fiddled with his braid as he fiddled with his words. "You won't let him convince you to go behind my back again?"

I frowned at him.

Before, when he found out that I went looking for demons, looking for my dad, behind his back, he hadn't been happy. He'd been upset to tears when he confronted me about it. Yet he'd forgiven me. It had almost seemed too easy then. Maybe that was because it had been. Maybe he hadn't actually forgiven me completely for it, and now he didn't fully trust me not to repeat the same mistakes.

I stood up and clenched my fists. "I said I wouldn't. What, you don't believe me? I told you, I wouldn't lie to you again. I promised I wouldn't go out looking for trouble. I'm not going to go back on it."

"Ava, I didn't mean that—"

"Then what did you mean?" I snapped, snatching my hand away from his.

I looked down at my fists. The tips of my fingers had gone black. How could Chay think that? I'd promised. I told him Kaiden was the one who'd gone after the demons, and I had nothing to do with it. That I talked to him. Why would I let Kaiden go and convince me to do something so careless right after warning him not to?

Chay didn't trust me. That thought made my arms quake, my fists clench tighter. I guess that made us even, though. I didn't trust him, either. I didn't trust him not to get in too deep and get hurt.

That's all he was afraid of, too, though, wasn't it? We were both afraid the other would get hurt.

"I just think Kaiden can be a bad influence on you, that's all." Chay stretched out his hand, stopping short of touching my knuckle, where the ash and ember had traveled upward. "Ava... I'm sorry. It's okay."

If I was too angry, things tended to burn. Chay was considerate of that and gave me the needed space. He was so attentive to my needs, it made my heart ache. He was too good for me. After glancing down to make sure my fingers weren't about to combust anymore, I reached out and took his hand, placing it on my cheek.

"I'm sorry, too. I know you're just worried about me. I worry about you, too, you know. Being out there, fighting crime."

He stroked my cheek. "I know."

"Can't you just...stop being Falcon? Like I stopped being Raven?" I pleaded with my eyes, with all my being.

There was hesitation in his eyes. A glimmer of regret, of guilt. The answer was no. Of course it was.

"I... She told me to do good, with this power. I should use it. To help people."

Right. Chala. The lady who'd given him the earrings. All he'd told me was she said something like 'with this, you will do good' before she passed away. Seemed awfully rude not to explain something so vague and cryptic. It wasn't really my place to judge, though. That'd be disrespectful to Chay and to her memory.

I sighed and looked away from him. "You don't have to be a superhero to help people. And the demons are still out there."

The mood of the room had dropped so low I could practically feel a chill in the air. I rubbed my arms and fell back on my bed.

"It's dangerous," I said.

Chay leaned over me and splayed a hand on my chest. I put my hand over his.

"I'm strong. I can take care of myself."

I held his hand tighter. "But you're no match for them."

His face fell. I didn't like it when he looked so melancholy. I'd much rather see him smile. He didn't say anything else, instead leaning down to kiss me, softly, cautiously at first, until I returned the kiss, a silent reply signaling to him this was okay, that it was fine with me to continue.

He threaded his hands through my hair and slipped onto my lap, deepening the kiss. We both inhaled sharply, like we were bracing for impact. I thought about how we'd been stopped before. I thought about how Chay should be studying, how I should be studying, and whether that really was more important than this, than just being with Chay, feeling him close.

I wasn't sure I was ready for anything else yet. I just didn't want to lose Chay.

"Can we lie on our sides?" He asked, barely a whisper against the kiss, making my lips tingle.

I nodded and we turned on our sides, facing each other. He continued to kiss me, feather light brushes of his lips against mine and along my jawline. His hands trailed down my chest, then dipped up my shirt. Every time since that terrifying moment, the intimate moments felt heavier to me, more desperate somehow. It was as if every heartbeat could be our last. And I didn't have many heartbeats left. I felt as if I couldn't waste a single one. I cupped his cheeks as I kissed him back.

"Roll on your back?" I said, though it came out as a

request rather than an order. Chay smiled that sweet smile, gave a nod, and rolled over. I moved so my knees were on either side of him, looking down on him.

I remembered a time when we were in a similar position, only fighting as Raven and Falcon. It seemed like another lifetime, yet it was only a few months ago. I hoped the next few months would be less eventful than these past few. I wanted that boring nose-in-the-books college life. I wanted those cool nights cuddled up in bed with my boyfriend. I wanted to be a boring, simple, college student with Chay, damn it.

Except I couldn't, because he was still a damn superhero.

"Ava?" He held out a hand for me. I took it and leaned in, pressing my forehead against his. "You okay?"

"Yeah. Fine. I'm fine. Just... Nevermind. It's silly."

"I'm sure it's not." He squeezed my hand and rubbed his thumb across it, giving me a peck. "You can tell me anything, and I promise I'll never think it's silly."

"Okay..." I sat up and stared down at him. "I want us to be normal, boring college students. I want to do all the boring shit that couples do together. With you. I just want to be with you."

"Ava..."

I put a finger over his lips before he could say something to ruin this ridiculous confession of mine. "You feel like home. I don't want to lose you. Please. Just. Stop doing the superhero thing and be a boring college student whose biggest problem is how much he freaking loves his boyfriend?"

Chay smiled wide. "I would love nothing more than to be boring boyfriends."

Wait, it worked?

Was I grinning like a big love sick puppy right now? I totally was. "Good." I touched his cheeks and closed the gap between our lips again, more passionately than before. He grabbed onto my arms, held onto them like his life depended on it. My heart clamored in my chest, screaming at me for more, telling me to never ever stop loving Chay. I didn't plan to.

This was all I wanted. Some silly domestic relationship with the guy who'd dropped into my life and shown me not everyone was an asshole out to get me. Who'd shown me how to love. Who'd accepted me for who I was.

We turned on our sides and kept kissing. Chay worked his hands under my shirt again, feeling my chest, and I wondered if he could feel just how hard my heart was beating. To me, it was like it was on fire and going to jump right out and attack him like Raven, at one point, would have done to Falcon.

"Want it off?"

I nodded. I couldn't form words right now. I lifted my arms so he could pull my shirt over my head.

"Mine, too?"

I gave another nod. "Yeah." I managed to say, nearly croaking.

He took his off, and I stared at his smooth, copper chest. I touched his heart and ran my hand down. Right where... I winced.

No, don't think about it again. You were doing so good.

"Are you okay?" Chay asked, likely seeing the wince of pain as it shot across my face.

"Yeah. I'm fine. Are you fine?"

"Yeah. I'm good." He touched my cheek and brushed some hair back from my face, though it did no good because it flopped right back where it was. For a moment he touched

33

noses with me, before turning his head and leaning the rest of the way for a kiss.

I returned the kiss and pushed him back down on the bed. I tried to get lost in the kiss, but the moment had grown into this heavy burden again, that one single terror permeating my thoughts and intruding on any ounce of pleasure I hoped to get out of kissing Chay. It always intruded at the worst time, and ruined everything.

I tensed up, pulled away, and stared into his eyes.

"What's wrong?"

I shook my head. "Does it...still bother you?" I looked down at his chest, and so did he.

He took my hand and placed it over his heart. "Feels like it never happened."

I leaned my head against his and closed my eyes as relief rushed over me. "Good." The most terrifying moment of my life so far had been when I thought I might lose him, and not just because I was leaving. Every moment now I was afraid and waiting for things to implode or explode. But he was fine. Chay was fine.

Like it never happened. Not even a scar.

We just lay there after that, until it got late and Chay needed to head out to get some homework done.

CHAPTER FOUR

CHAYTON

I WASN'T SURE what to say after Ava's question, and I guessed Ava wasn't either.

Does it still bother you?

I told him it felt like it'd never happened, but that was just on the outside. Inside, I was still sinking, still hurting. The scar wasn't visible.

I headed back to my room and tried to concentrate on my homework. I checked my phone and saw a message from Dy: *Are you doing okay?*

Yeah, I'm fine, I replied. I hadn't called him yet. I should probably do that, so I added quickly: *I can talk now if you want, sorry it's so late.*

He immediately replied: *Sure.*

I pressed call and he picked up after barely a ring. "Hey, coz," Dy answered in his low, firm, yet welcoming voice.

"Hey, Dy. Sorry I got caught up with my homework and forgot to call." Again, I was speaking in half truths. I felt a pinch of guilt for that.

"No problem. Are you doing okay?"

"Yeah, I'm fine. Keeping busy." My voice didn't come out as reassuring as I'd hoped.

"You think you'll want to come home for spring break?"

I immediately winced at the thought. I hadn't been planning to. I hadn't come back during winter break, either. I'd spent it with Ava and I planned on spending spring break with him, too.

"I dunno. I thought I'd stick around campus, actually. It's only a week." Should I tell him about Ava, I wondered? The words caught in my throat again. *He wouldn't care. He knows I'm queer.* But it wasn't that.

"Are you sure? I can help pay for a plane ticket."

"No, you don't have to do that. Save your money, Dy." I couldn't take from him any more than I already had. Dy had helped me so much already. I wouldn't be here if it wasn't for him.

"Okay, if you're sure. If you need anything, let me know. I'll talk to you again soon."

"I will. Later, Dy." I hung up and sighed.

I reminded myself I needed to try to be more responsive, so I wouldn't worry him like I had when Chala passed away. He might think I needed to be dragged out of my depression again.

I tried to refocus on finishing up my homework, managing to make some progress, though not as much as I would've liked. Jossia came in just after I finished my homework, gave a brief greeting, and we settled down to sleep for the night.

AVARI

THE NEXT MORNING, I texted Kaiden a big *WTF*.

Kaiden replied: *What?*

What do you think you were doing? I thought we agreed, no going after demons.

Kaiden: *I said *we* wouldn't ;P*

I'm going to kick your ass.

Kaiden: *I'll be right over! ;D*

I groaned. More than likely, he freaking meant that.

Sure enough, just a few minutes later he burst through my door, without even knocking.

"Here for my ass kicking!"

I stood up, growled, and shoved him backwards. He fell onto my bed giggling.

"I like where this is headed," he said, winking and sticking his tongue out at me.

"I was damn serious, you know. What the hell, Kaiden?"

"What? I don't see what the problem is. You said you didn't want to fight them, and stay safe. If *I'm* the one fighting all the demons, aren't you staying out of it?"

I grabbed his shirt and pulled him up, leveling my glare on him. I wouldn't normally let my face be this close to his, or anyone else's except Chay's, but I was done playing nice. I could taste his breath on mine, but I shoved down the urge to move away and held my ground.

"That's not what I meant, and you know it. I need you to

stay out of trouble, too. If you keep fighting them, they could keep coming."

Kaiden shrugged. "I doubt that."

"How do you know? Since when are you an expert on demons?"

Just because Kaiden had like, really far removed demon blood, that didn't make him the expert authority on them. He hadn't even known about being part demon until my dad said something to him.

"Well, I can sense them, for one thing."

"You...What?" I loosened my grip on his shirt. "Like my dad could?"

"Oh, damn, your dad could sense them, too? That's sweet!"

If I could sense them, too, maybe I could keep tabs on them, make sure that the demon activity was decreasing in the area... I hadn't had the chance to ask my dad how to sense them.

"Can you teach me how?"

Kaiden grinned. "Maybe."

"Can you or not?" I growled.

"For a price." His grin turned mischievous. I didn't like where this was going. I figured Kaiden would want something out of it. Couldn't he put his self-absorbed selfishness aside for one second?

"What?" I clenched my teeth together and gave him a threatening shake.

"Take me flying!"

I let his shirt go and turned away, crossing my arms in contempt. "No way."

"No lessons, then."

I needed to learn how to sense them, for Chay's safety, and my own. If I could sense when there was a threat, or if the demons were moving out of the area, I could protect everything I held dear. One little flight could cost me everything, though. Even if I wanted to so badly myself. I needed more time before I did anything rash, or else I might run into trouble. The demons were still here.

"You can be such a little shit, you know that?" I sneered at him.

Kaiden grinned back at me. "Come on, it's just one little flight. It won't hurt anything."

"Don't you get how dangerous 'one little flight' could be? Or did you forget how we ran into trouble so easily before?"

"Pff, you worry too much. It's not like we couldn't handle them if we did get into trouble. Or did you forget how we're a deadly duo of knives and fire?" Kaiden jeered back at me.

I let out an exasperated sigh and facepalmed. "You are hopeless."

"Aw, but—"

"But nothing." I reached out and hauled him up by his shirt collar, shoving him towards the door. "Leave."

"Ava—"

"I said *leave*. I'm not negotiating with you just so you can get your kicks, Kaiden." I shot him a hard glare.

Kaiden sighed and threw his hands up. "Okay, okay. But consider this." He swirled around and his eyes lit up with inspiration. "If you want to sense them, we'll have to be closer to one."

I narrowed my eyes at him. He did have a point. Still, I couldn't be caught out in the skies, where the demons might be lurking.

"We walk off campus. No flying."

"No way! We might not be able to find any that way! They've been getting further and further away!"

My scowl deepened. "We don't need to find them, we just need to be close enough to sense them."

"Well, there's probably not any close enough, boss. Do you want to take the BART?" Damn it, Kaiden. He had a point. I *did not* want to take public transit.

"Hell no."

I already had nightmares about the one time I went with Chay, and if it hadn't been for him being there, I might've had a meltdown. Kaiden, with his abundance of energy and incessant gabbing, which could sometimes actually be a welcome distraction from my haunting thoughts, would likely be stressful and give me a sensory overload in that environment. More than likely, he'd start babbling on about something he really shouldn't be with all those people around, then I'd have that to worry about, too.

"Well, then." Kaiden grinned his shit-eating grin at me. "My offer stands. And with good reason. We gotta fly somewhere to get a reading on the demon radar, boss."

I sighed. "Fine, fine." I grabbed at his shirt again and gave him my best stern look, trying to embody Falcon's commanding energy. "No funny business. We're trying to sense them only."

"Okay!" Kaiden beamed and pulled out of my grasp to skip towards the door. "Let's go now!"

"Ugh. Now? Can't we at least have breakfast, first?" My stomach growled as if to drive home my point.

"Oh, right! We should totally grab something over in SF! Oh, I know! Have you ever hit up Japantown? There's a kick ass taiyaki place there that I think you'd love!"

"Taiyaki? What's that?"

"Oh man, we *have* to go, now! They're like fish shaped stuffed waffles."

"Okay, that does sound good." Leave it to Kaiden to

bribe me into the busy city for food. But he'd piqued my interest. Food was the way to my heart.

"This is gonna be so AWESOME!"

I sighed and headed out the door. "I mean it, no funny business."

Cutting through the grassy areas to avoid the throngs of the morning rush on campus, we made our way, me snapping my fingers idly and Kaiden rambling on about whatever (I think he was describing Japantown to me). We arrived at my favorite, usually deserted, patch of trees. Climbing up in the camouflage of the leaves and taking off from the top of the tree was satisfying in a way I couldn't explain.

"Raven and Slash, together again!" Kaiden said and bounced on his feet.

"Shut it," I barked. "Don't get any ideas. This is not a Raven thing."

He pulled two masks out of his pockets, as if he hadn't listened to a damn word I just said.

"In case someone sees us. You want to play it safe, right?"

"Don't talk to me about playing safe. You're the one who's going out on his own fighting demons. You're hopeless," I said and shook my head at him.

I snatched the black mask away from him anyways, because whether I liked it or not, he was right. After a quick glance around to ensure the coast was clear, I removed my shirt, looped it through my belt, and slipped on the mask.

"I'm just so excited! And you look so cool! I've missed seeing you in action."

"No one said anything about me being in action. We're just going flying. No fighting, no funny business. Got it?" I gave him a hard look before hopping into the tree.

"Yeah, yeah." He grunted as he climbed up after me. Damn Kaiden. He wasn't one bit intimidated by me. Part of me wished Chay was here to give him some of the magic Falcon glare. That'd set him straight. I didn't want to bring Chay into this, though. I couldn't risk it.

"Just get your damn mask on," I said as I did so myself.

He giggled, though I didn't find anything about this amusing, and pulled the mask on.

I sighed and accepted my fate as Slash's object of amusement. At least I was getting something out of this. Hopefully.

Slash put his arms out and beamed at me. "Take me away, masked man of mayhem!"

Hopeless. He was completely hopeless. I scooped him up and took off into the air.

"Woohoo!" Slash shouted, thrusting a fist up at the sky and nearly decking me right in the jaw.

"That's my ear. And watch where you're thrusting that fist, unless you want me to drop you."

Slash laughed. "Yes, boss," he said, disingenuously. If I were actually his boss, he'd listen to me, instead of half listening and not obeying. Hell, if I were the boss of him, he'd be fired, because he was the worst sidekick of all time ever. "I'm just so excited!"

"Stop wiggling."

We flew over the Oakland Bridge. Normally I might pause and take a load off there, admire the view for a bit. Breakfast was on my brain, though, and I wanted that taiyaki thing Kaiden had mentioned. So, I pressed onward, past Treasure Island and towards San Francisco. The air chilled me through, at least the parts of me that Slash and his oversized bright orange hoodie weren't touching. He held onto me tight when I shivered. I didn't particularly like being so close to him. It wasn't the worst thing in the entire world, but I couldn't wait to land and have my personal bubble back for a few minutes. At least I wasn't cold all over.

"So, whereabouts is Japantown?"

"Around Geary! It should be just a little further ahead!"

I landed us in a patch of trees a couple blocks over. After resealing my wings and tugging on my shirt, I dropped down from the tree. Kaiden fumbled and half fell out of the tree, making me have to catch him in my arms.

"My hero!" Kaiden said with starry eyes. Our faces were entirely too close for my liking and I quickly righted him and pushed myself away.

"You're not graceful this morning," I mumbled.

"My foot slipped!"

"Be more careful," I grumbled.

"Sorry, I was excited!" Kaiden skipped forward, fully recovered from his slip up now. "Let's go!"

"So, how does it work?" I asked as we started walking. It was still early and the sidewalks were pleasantly uncrowded.

"What?"

"Sensing the demons?" I growled. He really did have a one track mind.

"Oh! Right. I just concentrate." I found the idea of Kaiden being able to concentrate on anything hard to believe.

"And?"

"I dunno."

I sighed. Hopeless. "What do they feel like?"

"It's hard to explain."

"Well, *try*," I snapped.

"Okay, okay. Calm down." Kaiden's brows pinched together as he took a moment to think. At least, I hoped that was what he was doing. "It's this really...imposing feeling? You know?"

"Imposing?"

Kaiden shook his head. "I don't know. It just feels bad. Unpleasant. Like I ate something rotten."

"Evil?"

"Yeah! That's it! It feels evil."

"That's what my dad said, too. It's like pure evil."

"Yeah! It's weird at first, but you'll know when you feel it. It's like nothing else I've ever felt. It happened a lot as a kid, you know. Eventually I connected it to when demons came around."

"You've been able to feel them for that long?"

"Yep!" Kaiden grinned at me, obviously pleased with himself. He had my complete attention, and I had no doubt he was on cloud nine because of it. "You know, come to think of it, why didn't you see any as a kid, Ava?"

That was a good question. I wondered for a moment before coming to a conclusion. "You know, I'm not sure. But I think, maybe, it had something to do with my dad. He mentioned to me he usually kept the demons away from this area, that is, until I started causing mayhem."

"That makes sense! I only saw a few as a kid. Must've been like, the stragglers."

"I guess so. I probably wouldn't have noticed them anyways. I've always been lost in my own thoughts."

"You think too much!" Kaiden said, giggling.

I chuckled myself. "And you don't think enough." I bumped shoulders with him.

We walked through the scenic Japanese-style plaza and into the open area mall. Kaiden led me to a quaint coffee shop with a wooden sign above it that said "TAI YAKI".

"They have red bean, chocolate, and banana!" Kaiden

said cheerfully.

"Oh, you know what I'm getting."

Kaiden chuckled. "Chocolate fiend."

"You know it." I grinned and ordered three chocolate taiyaki along with a banana and a red bean just to try them, and some tea.

Kaiden ordered one of each. Once we both had a plate of steaming fish shaped delights and tea, we took a seat nearby. It was still somewhat early, so the people were sparse here.

I bit into a chocolate one and hummed with delight, reveling in the chocolatey, fluffy, sweet goodness.

"Good, aren't they?" Kaiden beamed at me, obviously pleased with himself.

"Heavenly." I took another bite, savoring the chocolatey delights. Something else occurred to me. "What about me? Can you sense my presence?"

"Yours?" Kaiden paused between bites and looked puzzled. "Huh, I never thought about that."

"My dad said that's why the demons started showing up."

"I guess that makes sense then! Maybe that's one of the things that drew me to you." Kaiden winked at me like it was something to joke about, but I thought it was a good point. It was probably true.

"I never asked you exactly how long you'd been watching me, come to think of it."

His grin turned more mischievous. He popped the rest of his red bean taiyaki into his mouth and spoke while chewing. "Long enough to know what you were up to."

I nudged my foot into his under the table. "That wasn't an answer."

Kaiden coughed and swallowed his food, then bumped

my foot back. "Wouldn't you like to know?"

"I would. So answer me." I glowered at him and stole his chocolate taiyaki off his plate.

"Hey!"

"That's what you get for being stubborn." I stuck out my tongue at him before biting into the stolen taiyaki.

Kaiden pilfered my red bean one, which was no real loss to me, and stuffed it into his mouth, making a pouty face. "Fine. Beginning of September."

So, basically the whole damn time. I should have expected as much from him.

"Damn stalker." I grumbled and kicked at his shin.

"Ouch!"

I gulped down my now cold tea and stood up. "Let's get out of here."

"Aw, but I'm not done yet!" Kaiden whined.

"Eat and walk." Without waiting for him, I started walking. Only a second later Kaiden was stamping after me.

"Wait for me!" He said with his mouth full.

CHAPTER FIVE

AVARI

I PERCHED US on the Golden Gate. The view was spectacular up here; it was one of the first places I flew to when I started going out flying regularly. Though my recent memories had soured it somewhat, it still was one of my favorite places. I made a difficult choice up here to leave everything behind, and I'd almost followed through with it. Even though I ultimately couldn't leave everything behind, couldn't leave *Chayton* behind, it still stung to recall how I almost had. Twice. Never again.

"Ah! I'll never get over how cool this is!"

I scoffed fondly. "Yeah, it's pretty cool getting to see all the different angles and views up there that the designers never expected a normal person to see. It's beautiful."

"I never thought of it that way! Are you into design?"

"Not really. I just like admiring the architecture. I almost pursued it when I was younger, but I'm not much of an artist. I'm more into the mathematics of it all, so I went the engineering route."

"Yeah, I've seen your handwriting, dude." Kaiden giggled.

"Pff." I elbowed him, lightly because we were up high and I was not keen on the idea of rescuing Kaiden from a deathly fall. "Artists can have bad handwriting, too. *You* should know that." I'd seen his notebooks and chicken scratch on his walls.

"Touche, man." Kaiden gave me a sheepish grin. "If we could combine my artistic ability with your wicked math skills, I bet we could make a badass structure."

I chuckled. "I bet we could." More than likely I'd just spend hours upon hours telling Kaiden how mathematically impossible his designs were, but the thought amused me, still. I'd only been in his room a couple times, and from what I could tell from his scattered sketches and paintings, he mostly did abstract art, so I doubted he could *actually* design a decent piece of architecture, either.

"We'll add it to the bucket list!" He grinned.

"We have a bucket list now?"

Kaiden shrugged. "Why shouldn't we? All besties should!"

I shook my head and gave a dejected sigh at his ridiculousness. "Whatever. So, do you feel any demons?"

"Oh, right. Demons. Let's see here..." Kaiden closed his eyes, like he was concentrating. I certainly hoped he was. "I got something!"

"Yeah?"

"Let's go!" He started to stand, but I planted a hand on

his shoulder and held him down.

"Not so fast. We aren't chasing after demons, I told you. How do you feel them?"

"Close your eyes and try for yourself!"

"Okay..." I closed my eyes, unsure what else exactly I was supposed to be doing. I thought of my dad's words, about how they felt evil. "I don't feel anything."

"Try harder. Think of it like reaching out, like you're seeking it, not waiting for it to come to you."

Like I was seeking it. Okay... I imagined an invisible hand that reached out and felt for the presence of... well, evil, whatever that felt like. I came up empty again and sighed, again, unsure what it would feel like if I got it right. My head just hurt from the effort of pinching my brows together. It was more like I'd just been banging my head into a wall over and over.

"I still don't get it. What do you do?"

"I just close my eyes and feel it!"

I opened my eyes to narrow them at him. "Be more specific. There's got to be more to it."

"Hm." Kaiden rubbed his chin in thought, I presumed, though I wasn't holding my breath on that one. "It's just so natural to me, I guess. It feels like...prickly? Kinda like I'm being watched!" I rolled my eyes at him. His descriptions left much to be desired.

"So helpful," I mumbled and closed my eyes again, trying to reach out with an invisible hand and feel for something "prickly" as Kaiden said, or like I was being watched. I tried actually putting out my hand when that didn't do anything. My fingers started tingling a moment later. "I think I feel something."

"Yeah?" Kaiden snorted.

"What?" I opened my eyes and saw his fingers hovering

around the tips of mine, just barely touching them. I grimaced and slapped them away. "Asshole."

Kaiden laughed. "Sorry, you were just being so serious, I couldn't help myself!" He cackled.

"*You* should be more serious."

His mischief-filled grin told me there would be no seriousness from him, probably not ever. I shouldn't have expected anything less from the disaster that was Kaiden.

"Let's try to tell what direction they're in!" Kaiden suggested and closed his eyes.

"O...kay..." I wasn't quite sure how to do that, so I just closed my eyes, too, thinking of the hand reaching out. *Seek it out*, I thought, and held out my hand after taking a quick peek at Kaiden to make sure he wasn't up to his antics again. *Where are you, demons?*

Still, nothing.

"Whaddya think, captain?"

I shrugged. "I got nothing."

"To the north! Try turning that way and feeling again."

I gave him a reluctant stink eye, but turned anyway, and put my hands out again. *Evil, evil... Come out, come out, wherever you are.* I growled when I still came up empty handed.

"How far away do you think they are? Can you tell that, too?" I asked.

"Kind of. They'll feel more overbearing and intense, the closer you get to them."

"Hm." I closed my eyes and focused my reach north. My belly churned, though I wasn't sure if it was the sugary breakfast or just my imagination.

"We should get closer!" I opened my eyes and gave him a skeptical look. "You want to be able to tell how close or far away they are, don't you?"

"Yeah..." I sensed I was playing right into Kaiden's hands again, and I wasn't sure I liked where this was going.

"Then come on! It can't hurt anything."

"I don't know..."

"Oh, come on! You might feel them if we're closer!"

I sighed as I resigned myself to my fate. "Fine. But don't you dare go running off. Sensing only."

"Eee!" Kaiden threw himself at me as soon as I stood and I struggled to pick him back up.

"You've *got* to stop doing that, or so help me, next time I'll drop you."

Kaiden giggled. I scowled at him, unamused.

I flew to the north. This time, I tried to sense with my eyes open. My brows furrowed as I attempted to feel something, *anything*, and failed.

"Can you tell if we're getting closer?" Kaiden asked.

"No," I groaned.

"Land around here!"

I lowered us down on a rooftop and gazed around. There was nothing in the air, and I couldn't *feel* anything either. I was extraordinarily horrible at this.

"There! I see them!" Kaiden scrambled out of my arms and pointed down at the street.

There were two of them, casually walking along the street, almost as if they were people. Demons didn't move like people, though. Their movements were slower, stiffer, and somehow sinister. Maybe it was their charred looking skin, or their blood red eyes. It never failed to send chills down my spine.

"I'm going after them!" Kaiden said, and started climbing down the ladder on the side of the building.

"Like hell you are! Kaiden, get back here!"

He grinned at me as he shuffled down the ladder and I

just missed getting a grip on his shirt. Damn him.

This was a bad idea. Kaiden never listened to me. The cost of this little venture had been too great; I'd been had. My hands shook, and I clenched them into fists, seething. *Damn it, Kaiden.*

He dropped down the rest of the way, slipping his mask on, and running across the street. I couldn't go after him, or I'd be breaking my promise to Chay. I absolutely couldn't be seen. Things were already bad enough. Kaiden was on his own. *I can't interfere*, I told myself, and yet I perched on the edge of the building, anxious.

He walked right up to the demons, whipped out a dagger, and shanked one right in the chest without a second thought. They were monsters, nothing more, so they didn't deserve any kindness. Still, it disturbed me how easily Slash got into this, how precise, concise, and cold he was to the violence. The knife piercing through the demon's chest brought back flashes of that moment I still couldn't forget. Slash's smirk was a stark contrast to my rising panic.

At least the monster was on the receiving end of this attack. But Slash couldn't keep doing this. One day, he'd run into a demon that wasn't just a prowling bottom feeder, and it'd be too much for him, and he'd end up skewered just as Chay was, and damn it, I couldn't let that happen. He was my friend. My annoying friend, but still, my friend.

Slash may think he was helping by doing this, but in truth, he was making things worse. He was making things harder for me. I wasn't sure what he was getting at. Slash wanted to play the hero, or antihero I supposed, in killing that which he shared blood with. Maybe he was trying to prove something, or prove himself to me. Whatever the reason, it needed to stop. It *had* to stop. *I* had to stop him, before it was too late. In fact, I might be the only one who could. Usually, he didn't listen to my wishes. He was getting better, though, and I was pretty sure he cared about me, or he wouldn't keep coming around. So, maybe I would be able to break through to him.

Down below, Slash dodged the other demon's swipe, and then threw his knife right at its head. The knife missed, whirring past and narrowly missing an innocent bystander. So, his aim *wasn't* perfect. Damn, what if he hurt someone? Thankfully, when Slash started his knife flinging, people scattered and scampered off to avoid the onslaught. Slash lashed out with another knife, slashing the demon's neck open. It fell over, and moments later, started decaying and breaking down into ash.

"Yeah!" Slash cheered, loud enough for me to hear. I shook my head and sighed dejectedly. What was I going to do with him?

He retrieved his knives and grinned, looking right up at me. Damn it, Slash. I sunk down, hoping the people who hadn't run off wouldn't look up along with him and notice me up here.

"Wasn't that so cool?" Slash said as he hopped onto the roof.

"No!" I growled and stood up tall, glowering down at him. "What part of don't fight any of them are you not understanding? I need you to stay the hell out of trouble!"

"I'm helping! I told you, there's still so many of them around. I can't just *not* do anything."

"Why not?" I growled. "Why can't you just listen when I tell you not to interfere? I told you, my dad will handle it. Why can't you accept that? I don't get it."

"You're the one that doesn't get it! There are *too* many of them! They aren't dissipating from the area. What if it's too much for your dad to handle? What if..." He paused to sniff, tears brimming in his eyes. I flinched back, immediately regretting my outburst. This was the first time I'd seen him cry. "What if he tells you he can't get them away, and you have to leave?" So, that's what this was about?

"I'm not leaving." Not now, not ever. I wouldn't leave Chay. I took a step towards him without thinking when he sniffled again. It was awkward with him like this, and I instantly missed carefree Slash.

"You say that now, but what if you didn't have a choice? What if you *don't* have a choice, and this never stops?"

I sighed and touched his shoulder to make him look at me and hopefully listen. A simple gesture like this didn't squick me as much as it used to with him. "It will stop. Just...please stop fighting them. For me. If you really want me to stay, then stop this. Let my dad handle it."

My dad could handle it. He was far more powerful than me, and infinitely more powerful than a guy with freaking knives, no matter how good Slash was with them. He wasn't perfect; I'd just seen him miss. One wrong miss was all it'd take, and then I'd lose my best friend, like I'd almost lost Chay. My heart clenched at the thought.

Slash sniveled and wiped the snot from his nose, full on ugly crying. Then, his face went pale and his eyes wide, like he'd just seen something horrendous.

"What? What's wr—" He shoved me away abruptly, cutting me off. A second later, a large, red blur slammed into Kaiden.

CHAPTER SIX

AVARI

WHAT I NOW recognized as a demon's fist, which was at least twice as big as Slash, slammed right into him and sent him flying. The nightmarish beast had turned its sights on me now.

Shit, I thought, shooting up into the air and narrowly missing the demon's fist coming down to flatten me into a pancake. Why the hell was a greater demon here? I hadn't been doing anything to tip them off. Was Kaiden attacking the lesser demons pissing them off, or something?

I had no more time to debate that. The demon was stomping across the building at a snail's pace, which was merely a facade. That thing could move swiftly if it wanted to. Damn it. I couldn't fight this thing. I had to get to Slash and make sure he was okay.

I scanned the area and saw a shattered second story window across from the building we'd been perched atop. Behind me, the demon stomped once, twice, and then with a loud *whoosh whoosh* it took off into the air. I beat my wings harder and swooped through the window, breaking a few more pieces of glass as I came through.

Slash lay on the floor, bits of broken glass all over him and on the floor around him. It crunched under my feet, and I winced. There was a line of blood going down his face. This is what I'd been afraid of all along. One wrong move, one miss, one too many scuffles, and Slash would be on the receiving end of the demons' wrath.

"Slash!' I rushed over and lifted him up. His head bobbed. He was out fucking cold. "Come on, don't tell me I'm going to have to carry you." I groaned and shook him a bit. Nothing. I didn't like this lifeless version of Slash who didn't have a perky retort. *You can't do this to me.* My hand trembled as I pressed my fingertips to his neck. There was a pulse. This thorn in my side wasn't dead yet, and he wasn't dying on my watch, God damn it.

The building shook as the demon outside bashed into it. That was all it could do with as big as it was. The damn thing was blocking the way I came. This building was brick. The only way out was back through that damn window. The demon rammed the building again.

I had no choice. The only way I could get through was by force.

"Sorry, Chay," I muttered as I pulled the domino mask back out of my pocket and slipped it on, preparing for the worst.

I heaved Slash over my shoulder and stood up to face the gargantuan beast.

"You want a fight, you got one, tough stuff."

It wasn't like I could possibly make things worse at this point, anyways. If what Slash said was true, it hardly mattered. If these things were getting aggressive towards Slash, they might find me sooner or later, fire or not. A little fire wouldn't make a difference now, and it was the only way we were getting out of this alive.

I held up my hand and let the flames come, as fierce as they wanted. That persistent itch to burn something felt scratched and relieved almost immediately. I pulled my arm back like a pitcher on a baseball field and threw my fiery curveball of death through the window and towards the demon.

The thing made an ear shattering screech and fell back. It was enough of an opening for me to zoom through, so I took it. I spared a quick glance at the mammoth monster. It's chest was scorched and ashen. Good enough for me.

I took off, flying as high and far from the demon as I could and praying it had been injured enough to either keel over or not pursue me. Every few seconds I looked back, relief washing over me anew when nothing followed.

I was out of breath and my wings were practically on fire (but not literally) by the time I perched on the Oakland bridge.

"Hey, wake up." I jostled Slash.

He was still out like a light. There were shards of glass all over him, which had smashed against me when I carried him and made tiny scratches on my exposed shoulder and arm, the sting of which I was starting to feel with some of my adrenaline wearing off.

"Slash, wake up." I kept patting him on the cheek. Come on, you damn twerp.

"Hnghn..." He groaned, and relief flooded over me immediately. Thank God.

"Kaiden?"

His eyes fluttered open. "Raven... Why do you have two heads?"

Oh, boy. That wasn't good. "You hit your head pretty hard, didn't you?"

"Did I?" He squinted at me, looking perplexed, either by my words, or my perceived two heads, or both, I wasn't sure.

"Don't you remember? A huge ass demon smacked you through a window."

He giggled. "You have so many eyes."

I sighed. It was so like him not to take things seriously, even when he was gravely injured. "We're going to the hospital."

I didn't have any other choice. If he had a concussion, he needed more care than I could give him with the dinky first aid kit in my room.

"Going for a fly?"

"Yeah." I picked him up and took to the air again. He giggled more.

"So tired."

"Don't fall asleep. Keep your eyes open."

I landed us in the most discreet area near a hospital I could find and pulled our masks off. Kaiden slumped down against the wall when I tried to stand him up. Good enough.

"You probably should take your knives out of your pockets."

"All of your million eyes are equally beautiful," Kaiden said in a complete daze.

"Okay, guess you won't be any help."

As much as I hated to do it, I started rummaging through all his pockets, pulling out knife after knife, dagger after dagger. Damn, he kept way too many knives stashed.

"How many damn knives do you need?"

"I like knives. They're so shiny."

"Yeah, yeah. I know you do."

I stuffed the knives behind some garbage cans.

"Is it nap time?"

"No. Come on." I concealed my wings and pulled my shirt back on, then grabbed his hand and pulled him up.

"Are we gonna hold hands?" Kaiden beamed at me.

My intent had been to let go of his hand as soon as he was standing, yet now... I thought of that moment when Kaiden was lying on the ground, blood streaked down his head. I sighed and accepted my defeat. If this was the price for making sure Kaiden would get to the hospital safely, then so be it. Whether I'd like to admit it or not, I gave a damn what happened to him, and I wasn't ready to let go of him, or his damn hand.

"Tell you what, we'll hold hands the whole way there. All you have to do is stay awake," I said, giving his hand an encouraging squeeze that served as a reminder to myself that Kaiden was *here*, he was *breathing*, and he would be okay. At least, I thought he'd be.

"Yay!" Kaiden fell against me.

"Come on, you can do it." I walked us slowly the rest of the way to the hospital.

CHAYTON

AS SOON AS I got out of my morning class, I pulled out my phone and scanned the local news. This was my usual time to go out as Falcon.

My eyes went wide when I saw the headline of a fire that'd broken out in the east SF area. A fire suspected to have been started by Raven. I almost dropped my phone. My knees went weak, and I had to squat down for a moment. *Deep breaths, in and out,* I told myself as I held my head between my knees.

What the heck had happened while I was in class? I scanned the rest of the report with trembling, sweaty hands, and as I read, my blood only boiled. Slash—Kaiden—had also been there?

I hurried towards the edge of campus, practically running. Once I was atop a nearby building that I usually ditched my bag at, I slipped on my Falcon uniform and took off towards the scene of the incident without a second thought. I tried to call Ava but he didn't pick up. Dang it. What had Kaiden dragged Ava into? Why had Ava been out with Kaiden? These questions burned in my mind as I descended on the burning building.

I landed near one of the firefighters. From here, I saw the blaze was mostly leftover embers now.

"Was anyone inside?"

"Nah," they said, waving a dismissive hand. "Shame you didn't get here, sooner, though. It was that arsonist again. I thought he'd quit." They shook their head dejectedly and walked away towards the fire truck. Their words lingered like a burn.

I alofted on a nearby building, staring down at the scene. A window was shattered, and on the sidewalk below there was a small crater, as if something had fallen from the window. Nothing was in the crater, though. If I hadn't known about the existence of the demons, I would be perplexed right now. To everyone else, this scene looked like one of needless havoc.

I sighed and palmed my eyes. Why had Ava been fighting a demon? He was supposed to tell Kaiden to cut it out, not join him. Where were they now, I wondered? I pulled out my phone and saw I had a missed call and a voicemail from Ava. He must've called while I was flying.

"Hey, Chay...So, um...I'm at the hospital with Kaiden. There was a...situation. I wasn't planning on interfering, but Kaiden got hurt, and I had to step in. I'll explain the whole thing later. I'm sorry. You um, probably shouldn't look at the news. Please don't let it be on the news."

My hands were clammy and shaking by the end of the message. I tried to call him back, but he didn't pick up. Dang it.

I growled and shoved my phone in my pocket. "Ava, how could you do this?" It seemed like I was going to have to put my foot down and talk to Kaiden.

I wanted to give Avari a chance to explain, but he shouldn't have been in this situation to begin with. I clenched my fists until they hurt. Deep breaths, deep breaths, I told myself. It didn't help.

I texted Ava: *I got your message. As soon as you leave the hospital let me know.*

My hands were trembling so much I could barely type out the message. Getting angry now wouldn't solve anything. I couldn't wait to give Kaiden a mouth full, though, for dragging Ava into this. All he seemed to do was tempt Ava into dangerous situations, and Ava just *let* him every time. This was the last time I was letting Kaiden trick him.

Too little, too late. I was useless here, and too worked up to be helpful elsewhere, either. It was probably best if I just headed back to campus to wait for Ava.

All the way back to my room, all I could think about was what happened, what I'd seen, and how Ava could do this. After all we'd been through, after all my warnings. It had all been in vain. And now all I could do was wait for Ava to return to me and explain how he'd screwed up yet again and gotten himself into a mess because of Kaiden. I wasn't going to even start with Kaiden. Where to begin? When I saw him, I had half a mind to go off. If I didn't calm down, that seemed likely. I really needed to calm down.

When I finally got back to my room, I flopped down on my bed with an exasperated sigh and a half-hearted wave to Jossia. He raised a brow at me. Did I look that frazzled?

"Dude, you okay over there?" He flipped his curly hair as he looked up from the open textbook on his bed.

"Fine. Just stressed." I turned my head slightly so I wouldn't be muffled by my pillow.

"Midterms?"

"Mhm," I fibbed. I should've been stressed about that, but instead I was stressed about my boyfriend and his no good friend going out on a demon fighting spree.

"They're kicking my ass, too, man. Try to take it easy, okay?"

"Yeah, I'll try," I lied, again, as I pulled my clunky hand-me-down laptop from beside my bed and flipped it open. I plugged in headphones so I could listen to news reports without suspicion from Jossia.

I found a more in depth story about the happenings from earlier and read through it.

Witness reports state the knife-throwing menace who has been recently seen in convenience stores, parks, and other locations around the Bay area was seen frolicking down the street, flinging knives about at unsuspecting pedestrians. Shortly after running from the scene, he was flung from a building where Raven was seen.

Eyewitnesses say Raven threw the knifed menace through a window, then followed him inside, and was seen fleeing the scene with him flung over his shoulder.

Reports also came in that Falcon arrived at the scene shortly afterward. Firefighters managed to tame the flames left behind by Raven. It is unknown how Raven and the knifed menace are involved at this time. More on this as it develops.

There were already several comments left at the bottom. *"Why did Falcon even bother showing up? He's a worthless hero."* one said. Another, *"I bet they're all working together and it's some ploy to make Falcon look like a real hero."* I closed my laptop and shoved it away before my blood could boil any more, and rolled over to face the wall. This wasn't what I'd signed up for. I only ever wanted to help people. Now, I was being accused of being a phony and being called worthless.

Maybe I was just a useless phony, and they were right. Maybe it would be better if I gave it up. I curled into a ball and held onto my knees so tight my knuckles turned white. Ava's words came to my mind: *Stop doing the superhero thing and be a boring college student whose biggest problem is how much he freaking loves his boyfriend?*

I remembered what I'd told him. *I would love nothing more than to be boring boyfriends.* It was the truth. I would've loved nothing more. But it wasn't possible. That was only becoming more and more obvious as time went on. Even if I quit being Falcon, Ava seemed to keep falling into trouble. I felt helpless to pull him out of this growing hole he was digging for himself. The more I pulled, the further he dug, and the further I was pulled in after him.

No matter how much I loved him, if he wouldn't stop what he was doing, it'd all go up in flames, and trying to save him would only draw me into the fire. It would only work if both of us stopped. But what if Ava *couldn't*? I had to stop him—and Kaiden—before it was too late.

I moved my earbuds to my phone and turned on some ambient music. The soothing, earthy flutes did little to sooth my anxiety. I dozed off until my phone started ringing, making me jump up straight in my bed with a surprised gasp. The lights were out and Jossia was asleep like a baby. I pressed answer quickly before I could check who it was.

"H-Hello?" My voice came out groggy and confused.

"Chay, what do you think you're doing?" Dy's booming voice responded, full of shock and concern that immediately put me on edge and shattered the remains of my grogginess. He hadn't taken that tone with me since I was younger and reckless. What had I done, though?

"What do you mean? What's wrong, Dy?"

"You should have told me, coz." Dy sighed. "You could've told me."

"Told you what?" My gut churned, despite having no clue what Dy was talking about.

"Chala gave you something. A gift. Didn't she?" A gasp escaped me before I could stop it. "Chay, why didn't you tell me? You can talk to me."

Without even thinking I hung up on him. He couldn't be talking about that. He couldn't know. Could he?

My phone immediately buzzed in my hands and I jumped, dropping it on the bed. I thought it was Dy calling me back, but it was a text message, from Ava.

We're leaving the hospital now.

It was after midnight. I sighed. He was probably exhausted. I guessed our talk could wait until the morning.

I replied: *Get some rest. Meet up in the morning?*

Ava: *Ok.*

Little dots flashed like he was typing more for a moment, but he never sent another message. I thought about saying something else, anything else, but I couldn't bring myself to even type a 'love you' right now. I lay back down and didn't fall back asleep, my mind going wild with thoughts of Ava and Dy and all the things that had happened today. I fell into a deep, dark headspace that I hadn't been in for a long time.

CHAPTER SEVEN

AVARI

I SAT IN the stuffy waiting room, fidgeting and feeling like I was being watched the whole damn time. When Chay texted me back such a calm and to the point response, my anxiety only went further through the roof. I wasn't looking forward to that conversation. What the hell was I even going to say? *Sorry, Chay, but I let Kaiden drag me into trouble again. You were right.* Yeah, that should about do it. Then I'd just prepare for the imminent meltdown.

"Avari Terran?" A nurse said.

I stood and cleared my throat. "Yeah. That's me."

"This way please."

The nurse led me to the room Kaiden was in and through the curtain, then had me sign his discharge paperwork for him because he couldn't sign anything or make any major legal decisions for at least twenty four hours, blah blah blah.

Kaiden was propped up in the bed with a bandage around his head and a dazed smile on his face. He was probably hopped up on drugs.

"Hey," I said after the nurse left us alone, or as alone as we could be in a curtained off section of a room.

"Hi. I have a concussion."

I rolled my eyes. "I know you do." I wasn't enthused about dealing with a drugged Kaiden already. Maybe he'd be less reckless, though. That'd be a plus.

"My head hurts."

That earned a snort out of me. Even after a near fatal encounter he wasn't serious. Maybe that's what I liked about him; he balanced out my over-seriousness. "I'll bet it does. How are you feeling otherwise?"

"Like I was flung through a window."

"Well, you were." I couldn't help the begrudging smile from splitting over my face.

"Was I?" Kaiden gave me a curious look. "It's all so fuzzy."

"Yeah, you were." I reached out and planted my hand on top of his. Normally, I'd never do this, but damn it, Kaiden had me scared to death. "You scared the shit out of me."

Kaiden's eyes widened. "I did?"

"Well, yeah. You were knocked out. Shit, you could have died. Do you realize that?"

"And that would bother you?"

"Of course it fucking would." I squeezed his hand. "You're my friend. Don't ask me why, but you are. I care about you, okay?" I couldn't believe he was finally making me admit that *out loud*. But he deserved to know. I wasn't just going to leave him behind. I wasn't going to run off. Even if I almost had once, I wasn't going to now. I'd made up my mind. He didn't need to worry about that, or protect me. "I'm not going anywhere. So, stop going out looking for trouble. For me?"

Kaiden beamed and threw himself at me, flinging his arms around me and holding on too tight in a gesture that *had* to hurt him, but far be it from Kaiden to worry about himself, ever. "You really do care!"

I sighed and reluctantly gave him a pat on the back. It was the least I could do. "Yeah. Don't make me repeat it. And stay out of trouble."

"Okay."

I pushed him back gently and looked him in the eyes. "Promise me."

"I promise. Cross my heart and hope to die."

I placed my hand on his shoulder and narrowed my eyes at him. "No. No dying. Got that?"

"Got it. No dying. Just cross my heart, then." He smiled, almost as wide as he did when he was carefree, concussion-free Kaiden, and it reassured me a little bit. I hoped he meant what he said.

CHAYTON

SINCE I WASN'T sleeping, I tried in vain to finish up some homework, and then headed over to Ava's dorm building around eight in the morning, when I couldn't take it anymore. That was enough time. I could at least talk to Ava. Dy...I wasn't sure yet. He hadn't tried to call me back, or text, or anything, and that only frightened me more.

Guilt built in my gut when I had to knock a couple times.

Ava opened the door with bed-mussed hair, rubbing his eyes. "Chay. What're you doing here?"

"Sorry. I woke up early."

He stepped aside and waved me in, yawning.

"Yo, Chay!" Kaiden chimed in from Ava's spare bed.

I narrowed my eyes at him. After yesterday's stunt, I really wasn't in the mood to see or talk to him. It figured he'd be here, though. No doubt both of them had been exhausted, and Kaiden had probably gotten banged up enough to not be left alone overnight.

Still, the very sight of Kaiden made my anger rise. He was selfish, and saw fit to turn Ava's words to suit his own needs or wants. He was a bad influence on Ava, and I couldn't take it anymore.

"Hey," I said, only to Ava, not acknowledging Kaiden. If I said anything to him I might explode.

"I let him stay here so I could keep an eye on him. He has a concussion," Ava explained.

I looked at Kaiden briefly, seeing his bandaged head. A fresh pang of guilt shot through me. Only a little, though. He'd asked for it. "Tell me what happened." I crossed my arms and glowered at Ava without really meaning to. Ava winced in response.

"Come on, sit down. I'll explain everything." Ava sat on the edge of his bed with a sigh and rested his elbows on his knees.

Out of distaste for the idea of sitting next to *Kaiden*, who I was far more upset with than Ava, I sat on Ava's bed and looked at him, waiting.

"Okay. Explain."

Ava took a deep breath. "Okay. So, Kaiden knows how to sense the demons."

Kaiden chimed in immediately with, "Yeah! It's a pretty sweet trick!"

Ava continued, ignoring him, "And, I thought that might be useful to know how to do."

"Ava said his dad could do it, too! But since he's off who knows where fighting demons, he can't teach Ava, obviously, so—"

"Kaiden, be quiet," Ava snapped. "So, yeah, the deal was if..."

"Yeah, yeah, so, we went over to Japan Town, to this awesome taiyaki place—Have you ever had taiyaki, Chay? It's really good!—And we went to the Golden Gate from there for our first lesson!"

"...I took him flying, he'd give me a lesson in sensing demons."

"It's been so, so long since we went for a fly! It was just one little fly! And the view was AH-MAZE-ING!" Kaiden rattled on, rudely, without any concern for interrupting and talking over Ava constantly—how did Ava *deal* with this all the time? It was like he had a Kaiden mute switch, or something, because he just kept talking like Kaiden wasn't there.

I wanted to ask Ava how the heck he'd fallen for this obvious ploy, but I kept silent, vowing inwardly that I'd hear him out.

"We tried sensing demons from the Golden Gate, but I was getting nothing." Ava bit his lip and steepled his hands together. He was getting to the part where things went wrong, I was sure.

"You shoulda seen him furrowing his eyebrows, concentrating all hard to sense the demons. It was so fucking cute. Your boyfriend is adorable when he's concentrating, you know that? Oh, of course you know that!" Kaiden winked at me, and probably would have elbow nudged me if I were sitting beside him.

This was a joke and a game to him. I seethed and clenched my fists. Ava grimaced.

"I'm sorry, Chay. But we had to get closer."

"Yeah, so we headed north where I was sensing some demon activity, so that maybe Ava could get a better read on his radar!"

"We ended up spotting one, even though I still couldn't sense a damn thing, and then Kaiden…"

"When I saw the demons, I went and took care of 'em! I couldn't help myself!" Kaiden grinned, seeming pleased with himself about this.

"…like the freaking reckless mess he is, went off to fight them. But I didn't go after him. I waited on the roof for him to come back. I was trying not to get involved, I really was." Ava clenched his hands together tighter and exhaled as he rested his forehead against them. It almost looked like he was praying. I suspected if he were, it'd be that I wouldn't blow up at him. I was pretty sure Ava wasn't religious. We'd never talked about it.

"The demons were a piece of cake, of course. They were no match for me and my knives." Kaiden snickered and made a pow-pow movement with his hands.

"But out of nowhere this huge one came in and attacked Kaiden."

"This HUGE one came out of nowhere! I was still riding on the high from picking off the little ones, and I didn't sense it until right before it struck! That thing hit me so hard I went through a window!"

"I had no choice. I tried not to make too much of a mess,

but I had to save Kaiden. As soon as I had Kaiden and put a fireball through that thing, I took off."

"I didn't see Ava fight because I was out fucking cold, but I saw the news reports afterward, and man, he was such a badass! You should be proud of how well he dealt with that thing. He's my hero!" Kaiden clasped his hands together and gave Ava goo goo eyes, and it made me sick to my stomach.

I'd had it. I was about to boil over. Of course this was all Kaiden's fault. I shouldn't have expected anything less. But Ava—when the heck was he going to learn his lesson, and stop following Kaiden into danger?

"I'm so sorry, Chay. I know it was a bad idea, but I thought that if I could learn to sense the demons, it'd help me keep us safe."

I was clenching my hands into my knees so hard to keep from exploding right now. Ava's hand reached over, hesitating over mine.

"Ava was only trying to help, Chay! Please don't be mad at him!" Kaiden pleaded.

I shot up and balled my hands into fists at my sides. "Shut up! I'm so tired of you talking constantly! Do you *ever* shut up?" I let out a heavy breath. Kaiden winced back at my bellowing words.

"I—I'm sorry," he said, timidly. I didn't believe his words for one second. I didn't believe Kaiden had ever truly been sorry in his life.

"Is this all a game to you? You interfering could cost us *everything*. Do you understand that?" I stepped towards him, standing tall, ready to—I don't know what, something. Make him pay. Make him sorry.

Ava put his hands around one of my arms. It brought my anger level down almost instantly. What had I even been about to do? "Chay... Please, stop yelling. It won't happen again. Kaiden promised me. Crossed his heart and everything. Right, Kaiden?"

"Right, boss!" Kaiden saluted.

I exhaled deeply. Ava turned me towards him, and I let my head fall against his bare shoulder. Frustrated, relieved, tears welled in my eyes. I hated this. But at least, Ava was safe, and Kaiden—supposedly—had promised not to pull any more stunts like this.

"This could've been so much worse," I whispered against Ava's shoulder.

"Did I mention I have a HUGE headache? Concussions suck ass!" Kaiden said.

"I know." He rubbed my back. "I'm sorry. I didn't think it'd come to that."

Across the room, Kaiden stood suddenly. "Whoa, that was a bad idea!" He was swaying dramatically.

"Don't let it happen again." I lifted my head and put my hands on his cheeks, making him gaze up at me. "Stop letting him drag you into trouble. Please."

"Hey, lovebirds, if the talk's over, I'm starving! Can we go get breakfast?"

"I won't," Ava said. I sighed and leaned my forehead against Ava's. "Guess we've gotta take care of the kid, now," Ava mumbled.

"Yeah." I sighed and stepped away.

"Are we going? Are we?" Kaiden bounced on his feet.

"Come on, trouble," Ava said.

"Yay!" Kaiden pranced out the door ahead of us, chanting "Breakfast time! Breakfast time!" outside while Ava pulled on a t-shirt and jacket, sighing and rolling his eyes.

We made our way down the sidewalk, Ava and I holding hands and Kaiden following along, humming like he didn't have a care in the world.

"What're you in the mood for? Waffles?" Kaiden asked.

"Waffles are fine with me. Okay with you, Chay?"

"Yeah."

"Little Gem it is! Yay!" Kaiden bounced on ahead. Ava made no effort to match his pace, and neither did I. It really did feel like we were Kaiden's worn out, beyond done parents.

I was far more patient than Ava was. Being around Kaiden and his boundless energy, it was apparent why Ava always looked so done around him. There must be something he liked about him, though, if he didn't snap and set something on fire instead. I couldn't say there was anything I liked about Kaiden.

"What're you guys getting? I think I'll get something super chocolatey!"

"Pff. Damn copycat," Ava mumbled.

"Do you really trust him to keep his word this time?" I asked Ava, keeping my voice low even though Kaiden was several feet ahead of us.

"Oh, man! Guys! I found a flyer for a party during spring break! We should go! It says it's queer friendly, too!" Kaiden pranced back towards us waving a rainbow colored flyer that I recognized as belonging to the queer student support group.

"I think so. It doesn't look it now, but he got banged up pretty bad. He's lucky he didn't break any bones," Ava said, paying Kaiden and his rambling no mind, but smacking the flyer out of his face when Kaiden put it too close. Kaiden snickered and skipped ahead again, dancing around other students from the early rising crowd.

"I hope you're right."

Kaiden ran into Little Gem ahead of us.

I leaned against Ava while Kaiden ordered. "...chocolate syrup, and Oreos, and whipped cream. Oh! And cherries!" The worker looked overwhelmed at Kaiden's endless additions.

When Ava and I stepped up, they didn't even ask us what we wanted. We came here enough for them to know our orders.

"They should just name yours the Avari Special!" Kaiden said with a grin as he scooped up his overloaded waffle and bounced over to an empty seat.

That joke got a laugh from the worker, and an eye roll from Ava. I had to admit, it was true.

We sat down across from him and I leaned against Ava, poking half-heartedly at my food and yawning. I wasn't really hungry, too much anxiety making my gut churn. It'd been awhile since I lost my appetite. I remember Dy having to force me to eat three meals a day at one point, standing over my shoulder to make sure I ate at breakfast and dinner, texting me at lunch time to make sure I ate that, too. Ava hadn't pointed it out. Yet, anyways.

"Stop blabbing and eat," Ava said to Kaiden.

"Ouch! Don't kick me! I'm injured!" Kaiden whined.

"You didn't injure your foot so it's fair game," Ava retorted.

Kaiden replied, but his mouth was full so it was unintelligible.

"Are you tired?" Ava asked me when I yawned again.

"Just a little." I leaned against him more.

"We can ditch Kaiden and go ahead back to my room if you want. You can take a nap there."

"Hey! Dun leab meh!" Kaiden's mouth was still full.

"Well, hurry up then!" Avari groaned.

Kaiden stuffed the rest of his food in his mouth, even

though it was more like three large bites, and swallowed hard after chewing only a couple times.

"I'm done!"

Ava sighed. "You're ridiculous."

We stood and started heading back to campus. I kept leaning into Ava and holding his hand. If I napped in Ava's room, and slept in his bed, would I sleep more peacefully? I didn't want him to know about the nightmares... I was just so tired, though. I wanted a good rest.

"You're not really gonna ditch me, are you, Ava?"

Almost to the edge of campus. It wasn't much further now.

I looked up to the walk signal and froze. Across the street, three people stood. It couldn't be... I blinked a couple times, let go of Ava's hand, and rubbed my eyes. I must be seeing things, or daydreaming.

Dy was here? Along with our cousin Tah, and Ona.

"Chay? What's wrong?" Ava asked, but I was too focused on Dy and the other two crossing over to us.

"Dy."

"Huh?" Ava glanced at me.

"Dyami's here."

"Chay," Dy said, waving his hand. He smiled, but it didn't reassure me. I was too shocked that he was here.

"Yo, Chayton!" Ona beamed and waved at me.

"Hey," Tah said, not looking as thrilled as Ona, but Ona was always cheerful.

"Who's this?" Ava stepped closer to me, half between us.

I stepped around Ava, my nerves skyrocketing. "Dy? What are you doing here? Why didn't you tell me you were coming?"

"I got in last night. I was going to surprise you, for spring break, but..." Dy paused and glanced at Ava and

Kaiden.

"Chay?" Ava tugged at my hand. "Who is this guy?"

I bit my lip and glanced from Ava to Dy. "This is Dyami. He's my cousin."

"Cousin?" Ava's eyes went wide, and his head moved back and forth between us, as if he was trying to process this, to see the resemblance maybe.

Dy and I did look alike in some ways. We had the same strong jaw, a similar long nose. His lips were thinner, pursed in thought. He was older than me, in his late thirties, and his hair had started graying in the last few years, streaks of it along his temples.

"Who're these other dudes?" Kaiden chimed in. "Friends of yours from home, Chay?"

I ignored Kaiden, sharing an intense stare with Dy. He knew something. Something about my powers. I wasn't sure how much, exactly, but he *knew*. It made me shiver. Ona—who was wearing a "They Today" button— stood beside Dy, leaning against his shoulder and absently twirling a strand of their shaggy hair around their finger, smiling wide and staring off into space without a care in the world. Ona was always so carefree, a stark contrast to the current mood.

"Chay. We need to talk." He looked between me, Ava, and Kaiden. "Alone."

I swallowed.

"Who's undercut man-bun over here?" Kaiden said, stepping closer to my cousin, Tah. "Heylo there." I could practically hear his mischievous grin.

Tah uncrossed his arms and smiled crookedly at Kaiden, like he was...interested? I shuddered at that.

"I don't think so." Ava held onto my arm. "Anything you have to say to Chay, you can say in front of me, too." Dy glared at Ava like he wanted him to catch fire, ramping up my anxiety levels even more.

The intensity in Dy's eyes bothered me. Fear clawed at me from the inside, screaming at me to run, hide, avoid everything. Burrow under blankets and hide. That's what I wanted to do. I wanted to shut out the whole world and not deal with my problems.

"Ava..." I started.

"Kaiden, go home," Ava said.

"Aw why? I shouldn't be alone, what if I get dizzy or something? What's going on? Is some drama about to go down? You know I wanna be here for *that*!" Kaiden pranced away from Tah, who seemed crestfallen about that, and back beside Ava, bumping shoulders with him.

Ava sighed. "You're hopeless."

"Ava, it's okay. You can go with Kaiden. I'll come back to your room as soon as I'm done." It was better if Ava wasn't here for this. I wasn't sure how this was going to go, or what Dy would even have to say.

"Chay..." Ava gripped my hand tighter, frowning, eyebrows lifting with disappointment. "What's going on?" I wish I could answer that question.

"I'll be fine. Dy is family."

"Okay." He didn't look quite convinced, maybe because Dy was still glaring daggers at him, but he let go of my hand and looked to Kaiden. "Let's go."

"Aw, but this looks interesting." Kaiden whined, but followed Ava anyways, to my relief.

As Ava walked by Dy, he watched him like a hawk ready to strike. When he looked back at me, his glare had disappeared, replaced with an even, level smile that didn't reach his eyes. My stomach churned.

"Who are your friends?" Dy asked.

In all the confusion, I hadn't even thought about introducing them formally to each other. More than anything, I was wondering why Dy had come all this way out of nowhere. Had I worried him that much that he thought he needed to drop in for a surprise visit?

"The guy with the black hair is Avari. He's my uh...boyfriend. His friend is Kaiden."

"He's...what?" Dy's eyebrows raised, and his eyes went wide. But not in surprise. No, it was more...frightened. Shocked. Why would that frighten him?

"I'm sorry. I've been so caught up in college life, and we haven't been dating very long." It wasn't a complete lie, but it wasn't the truth either. It had been a hectic few months, but I also wasn't sure how to tell Dy about Ava. I was worried he'd pry or give me "the talk", or I'd slip and say something I shouldn't. So instead, I'd said nothing. Seeing how concerned he looked now had me questioning whether that had been a good idea.

"Chay... He's dangerous. You need to stay away from him."

An icy knife pierced through my heart as all the air left my lungs. What was he talking about? He couldn't know about Ava, too...could he? It was too late to play down my reaction and act like I had no idea what he meant by Ava was dangerous.

"Dy, Ava's not dangerous."

Dy stepped closer and placed his hands on my shoulders, brows creased deeply. "You don't know, do you? You don't know half of it." He gritted his teeth. "I should've come sooner. If I'd realized this..."

"Dy...what are you talking about? I—What don't I know?" My heart pounded harder in my chest as panic started to set in. This couldn't be happening. He couldn't possibly know... But why else would he be reacting like this?

"Chay, I'm so sorry. I think..." He squeezed my shoulders and took a breath. "I think you should come home."

My stomach plummeted, swallowed up by the chasm of my anxiety that had opened beneath me.

"What? Why?" I barely managed to speak; it felt like I was falling further and further into the chasm by the second.

"I thought it was safe here. I was wrong. I was *so* wrong. Come home, Chay. I have so much to tell you, and now that I know Chala chose you—"

"What are you talking about?" My breathing had quickened and my heart bashed in my chest. I stepped out of his grasp as I gasped for air against my constricting throat. What was he going on about? It wasn't safe here? Was this all because of Ava?

"You don't understand the dangerous situation you've put yourself in, Chay. Please, I don't want you to get hurt." He held out his hand to me.

The situation I've put myself in? I was flailing, falling, drowning, and though Dy was offering his hand, I wanted to shrink away from it and keep sinking. I didn't want to take it. I didn't want to go home. My place was here. With Ava. And Ava felt the same. What would he think when I told him this?

"Come with us, Chay. Together, we can do this. We can do what Chala wished of us." Dy smiled hopefully at me.

What Chala wished... Of *us*? Dy was reminding me of Chala right now. Always mysterious and vague, yet wise beyond his years. I thought of her last words to me: *With this, you will do good.* Lately, I'd been asking myself what exactly 'good' meant.

"Chay, please—"

"No!"

I turned away and ran, as fast as I could, even though I was being ridiculous and childish. I didn't want to deal with this. I had enough going on as it was. I just wanted to get away. Away from Dy, away from everything. I wasn't even headed back towards campus, I was so caught up in just getting away.

I wasn't sure I wanted what truth Dy had, about why I was in danger. I had this sinking, heavy feeling. I was drowning. I couldn't breathe.

I stopped running and dropped down, squatting by the fountain where I once had a conversation with Ava that I was pretty sure queued him in that I knew he was Raven, the Bay area arsonist, as the media had dubbed him.

I clutched my head between my knees and sucked in deep breaths. Everything around me seemed so loud. I just wanted it all to stop.

I didn't want to leave. Why did he want me to leave? After everything I went through to get here? I got out of the rez, unlike many of my peers and my parents. I had so much going for me here.

Why would he want to shatter that, after helping me get here? He was the one who drove me here to tour the university, for heaven's sake! After all that, now he wanted me to just up and leave?

My phone vibrated. I dug it out of my pocket with trembling hands and checked my messages.

It was from Ava: *We have a problem.*

CHAPTER EIGHT

AVARI

KAIDEN FOLLOWED ME all the way back to my room, the ever annoying nuisance that he was, blabbering all the while.

He was headed towards my bed, until I narrowed my eyes at him and jerked my thumb in the direction of the spare one. Without missing a beat, Kaiden grinned sheepishly and did a twirl, plopping down and flipping my TV on.

"Man, I wonder what was up with that!" Kaiden mused.

"I dunno."

I was more than a little worried about it, though. Where had his cousins come from? And what were they doing showing up out of nowhere? And why the hell had Dyami given me such a stink eye? He looked at me like he wanted to punch me. Well, if he was going to be a dick, the feeling was mutual.

"That one guy with the undercut man-bun was pretty cute, though."

"Huh?" I quirked a brow at him. He would be interested in something completely unrelated. "You're horrible." I sighed and rolled my eyes at him.

Kaiden shrugged. "I know what I like. Tall, dark, and mysterious." He waggled his eyebrows at me. "You know the type." He rolled onto his hands and knees and winked at me.

I shook my head disapprovingly, even if I laughed along. Kaiden giggled, then suddenly froze. His eyes went wide, and the color drained from his face almost instantaneously, like he just witnessed the gates of hell opening up before his very eyes.

Perhaps he had.

"Holy shit," he gasped out.

"What's wrong?"

"Man, you don't *feel* that?" He shot up and came to stand in front of me where I sat on my bed. "Try sensing for demons, boss."

"Okay..." I closed my eyes and focused all my effort on sensing for demons, thinking of reaching out like Kaiden had told me. A sharp stab of pain sliced through my head, and my ears rang. "Ah! Fuck!" I clutched my head and clenched my eyes shut tight. It was like a ten ton brick on my chest. It stabbed and wrenched and writhed and made me feel...wrong. Was this the demons? My knees and arms quaked uncontrollably at the intensity.

"Oh, what the fuck, man? Are you alright?"

I released my grasp on my head, grateful it was no

longer pounding, and looked up at him. "How the hell do you stand this?"

"I'm used to it, I guess?" Kaiden grinned and bit back a laugh. "Maybe you were trying too hard. I didn't think that'd happen, dude."

I sneered at him. "The hell is it? Do they always feel so...overbearing?"

"Nah, man. This one's HUGE. Probably the strongest one I've ever felt! And it's headed right this way!"

Headed this way? *No. No, no, no.* This couldn't be happening. What if it was that greater demon that I ran away from? Maybe it was bringing friends, too. My fingers trembled and I clenched them into fists to make them stop.

"Ava! We have to do something!"

"No," I blurted back automatically.

"It's gonna come straight here and smoke us out— literally—if we don't! We have to fight!"

"I said no!" I jabbed an arm out at him, clipping his side and sending him back a step. "You're staying right here. You stand no chance against that thing, and you still have a concussion. I'll take care of it." I had no choice if it was headed right for me, did I? Everything I did made things worse. For both Chay and myself.

"But I can help!"

I forced myself to stand, despite my legs still feeling wobbly. "No, you can't. The best thing you can do is stay put. I'll handle it." I jabbed my finger back at the spare bed. "You sit right here and behave. I'm not having you get hurt again."

Kaiden gave me puppy dog eyes and pursed his lip, but nodded. "Blow them out of the water for me?"

"I'll burn their asses back to hell."

I turned and strode out my door.

When I was outside, I texted Chay: *We have a problem.*

He might not reply, but I had to at least tell him that shit was about to go down. Every flame I hurled would only do more harm than good. Even if I killed the demons coming for us now, more would just come. More, more, and more. It was endless.

But why? Was my dad not drawing them away from the area? Or were there just that many?

My phone buzzed. Chay texted back: *What's wrong?*

There's some huge ass demons headed right for campus. I'm gonna draw them away. I'll try not to go overboard.

Chay: *Ava don't*

Even though he replied immediately, I didn't say anything else. There was nothing I could say. I had to do this. There was no other way. They would follow me. I had to protect Chay, Kaiden, and the campus from the demons. I wasn't going to let anything hurt the people I cared about. Not after I finally could say I had people I wanted to protect. I had something to fight for, and if I had to, I was going to fight.

Even though my hands trembled, even though my heart raced, even though I could hardly breathe, I would fight.

I leapt into the trees just on the edge of the dorms and peeled off my shirt and jacket, slipping on my mask as I took to the skies to meet my opponents. I reached out and felt for the demons, as best as I could. Kaiden was better at this. I wasn't going to bring him with me to get hurt again, though.

This time, it wasn't so overwhelming. Still, it was heavy on my chest, foreboding, wrong...evil. I flew in that direction, trying my best to press on despite the intense, evil pressure that loomed in the air.

They came into view just a moment later, three of them.

One of them was a greater demon, like I fought with my dad once before. That must've been the one I could get a read on. I swallowed a lump in my throat as I remembered that battle. If my dad hadn't been there to help me out, I wouldn't have been able to regain the upper hand.

I whistled at the demons and brandished a small flame on the tip of my index finger. "Hey, you shitheads! Over here!"

That seemed to work, and they loomed my way. I beat my wings hard, flying as fast as I could, only glancing back every so often to make sure they were still in pursuit. I just wanted them away from the campus, away from Chay and Kaiden. Whatever it took. I couldn't have demons banging down my door every few days, so if I could do this without too much fireworks, that would be preferable.

If I could get them as far away as possible, then deal with them with as little firepower as I could, maybe I wouldn't have more storming my castle the next day. Kaiden might have been onto something, trying to deal with the demon population on his own. This was getting out of hand, and from an outside point of view, it really didn't seem like my dad had a handle on anything at all. Where the hell was he? What was he doing?

I did *not* want this to turn into a regular thing. That boring college boyfriends thing was looking more and more unlikely.

Growling behind me alerted me that the demons were gaining on me. When I glanced back, they were almost too close for comfort. I sped up, did a loop de loop, and flung a fireball at one of the small demons, only for it to bat the damn thing away.

"Damn," I muttered, and sent another for it.

That one impacted its shoulder, and though it wasn't a

fatal blow, it did knock the demon for a loop. I flung another while the thing was caught off guard, which nailed it right in the chest. The demon wailed as its skin crackled, and it blew away in the wind. My eyes darted around, searching for the others. I spotted the other small one and hurled a couple flames its way. One hit and one missed, but it was enough to do the job.

Now, where was the—*POW!*

I spiraled out of control through the air after the greater demon slammed into me. My skull was pounding. I barely regained my senses before the thing rushed me again. I managed to dodge, just barely, and then hurled a fireball at it. The demon batted it away like it was nothing.

Damn. I needed more time to charge up a bigger flame to take this thing down. So much for not using a lot of firepower. The demon charged for me yet again. I veered out of the way and it went zooming by, then swooped upward sharply. Before I could turn, it was behind me and barreling into me.

The demon wrapped its arms around me. I gasped out as it squeezed, too tight, pressing my wings against my back and restricting me from breaking free. We started spiraling downward, just as the one before had. I was headed for that same fate I'd narrowly avoided once. Panic set in, and I wriggled desperately.

"Damn it! Let go, you damned thing!"

I growled and struggled, even tried bashing my head against the demon's, but that only hurt me, too. I wriggled and grunted. I was able move my hands, just enough to plant them on the demon and shoot it up with as much fire as I could. The demon jerked and loosened its grip on me. I broke free and went tumbling out of its arms onto the ground.

Shit, we were that close to the ground?

I sat up and stared at the demon. It was disoriented from crashing into the ground, but it was already recovering. I scurried to my feet as it was standing, and took off into the air again. I had to get more space between us so I could charge up a big attack, big enough that it'd blow this thing to smithereens. I hadn't wanted to, but it was the only way.

Just as I flipped around, I saw the demon spread its wings and start flying towards me. I opened my hands towards it and concentrated on bringing my fire forward — no, letting *it* come to *me*. That persistent itch felt scratched, my body whole and warm and full to the brim with fire, ready to burst free. I let it be free.

There was no time for the gigantic beast to dodge. My fire shot right through, making a gaping hole in its body, edged with cracked, burned embers. The thing hung for a moment, suspended midair, before falling back down, bashing into the concrete hard enough to leave a small crater.

I dropped my hands down to my sides and panted as the demon sizzled out and turned into ashes. I was so damn glad that was over.

Sirens blared in the distance, growing closer. Damn, had I really drawn that much attention? I wondered what they thought I was doing, or my dad, when they thought he was me. I stared down at the gaping crater of embers and ash. This did look pretty bad, no matter what my intent. I flew off before the authorities could make it to the scene, heading back to my dorm and trying to prepare myself for the worst.

I had just opened the can of worms, or more accurately, demons.

CHAYTON

I TEXTED AVA a few more times, while ignoring the texts coming through from Dy. I tried calling his phone, but it went to voicemail every time. Dang it.

He was gone, off to fight those monsters, and there was nothing I could do about it. I couldn't go after him, or else I risked my own life, flying into the midst of a battle I couldn't see raging. Not being able to see the demons, I wouldn't be able to help him. I would only be in the way.

So, I was stuck worrying over him. I was helpless. I was weak. I was a mess getting messier by the second. Anxiety was a raging beast in my belly, almost unbearable.

I settled for going back to his room to wait for him. I tried knocking, and sure enough, Kaiden opened up. I fought back a sneering frown.

"Oh, hey, Chay! Did you come to wait for Ava?"

"Yeah."

He stepped aside and let me in, flopping back on Ava's bed on his belly and planting his chin on his palms. Watching the TV intently, he swung his legs back and forth and hummed a tune absently for a moment before abruptly perking back up as if he'd had some epiphany.

"Oh!" He rolled off the bed and jumped to his feet, wavering a bit. "Whoa, shouldn't have done that, man!" When he recovered, he jabbed his hands outward towards Ava's bed. "You probably want that one, hm?" Kaiden grinned.

I maundered over to the bed, sitting on the edge with my legs and arms crossed, clutching my arms tightly and bouncing my foot anxiously. Meanwhile, Kaiden flopped onto the spare bed. Despite Kaiden's considerate act, he still annoyed me with his carefree attitude through this whole thing.

My hairs stood on end, and my fists clenched just watching him. Did he even care that Ava was putting his life on the line? Was he really so naive to think this was just some thrilling game with no stakes? He really peeved me off.

I was glaring daggers at him. I closed my eyes, centered myself, and tried to remain calm. It wouldn't do me any good to start some quarrel with Kaiden right now. All it'd do is rile up my nerves even more. Between worrying over Ava and what had just happened with Dy, I already had a wildfire of emotions burning through me, eating at the branches of my nerves. As if to drive home the point, my phone buzzed in my pocket. I yanked it out, saw it was Dy, and pressed ignore.

Kaiden turned up the volume on the TV. Ava—Raven— had made the news.

"A mysterious attack by Raven happened moments ago. Witnesses report Raven made the crater you see here, then fled the scene before authorities arrived. There was no sign of the hero Falcon, the Bay area's own superhero who has battled Raven in the past. Falcon has been appearing less and less in the past few months, as has Raven."

I stared at the crater behind the news reporter. This was exactly why I hadn't wanted Ava to go. It was beginning to seem like it was too dangerous for Ava. The thought of losing him struck me suddenly, tearing at my heart.

"Pff, maybe he's bored of normal superhero stuff like saving cats out of trees, without Raven." He rolled on his side, propped on his elbow, and smushed his cheek against his palm. "*Althoughhhh*. Wanna know a secret?" He beamed at me. Nerves still a mess and annoyance bubbling, I couldn't muster a reply. He continued without it. "I saw him recently. When I was out looking for demons!"

I had been at the encounter he was talking about, only as Falcon. I didn't dare look at him, though, or else I might reveal myself. He still didn't know, and I wanted to keep it that way. Kaiden had enough trouble keeping Ava's secrets. I kept my body as relaxed as I could, despite how on edge I was.

"I wonder who he is. Ava said he wasn't the same as him. But what's different?"

I simply shrugged. Normal Chayton wouldn't have any answers to these questions, at least by Kaiden's perception.

"You sure don't have much to say about Falcon, huh?" Kaiden rolled on his back and stared up at the ceiling. "I'm so bored!"

He really never stopped talking. I didn't have anything to say to him, so I kept my mouth shut and sat on the other bed to wait for Ava. I hoped Ava would be back soon. Without him, I was sinking into a miserable pit. At least if I were in his arms, maybe I could calm down. Like this, I had nothing to unrile me.

"Ah, Ava!" Kaiden blurted and shot up as soon as the door started opening.

"Ava!" I stood and rushed over to him before Kaiden could get in his face and immediately started looking him over. I touched his shoulders and stared at him. "Are you okay?" He didn't seem hurt, but I still asked to be sure.

"I'm fine." He held out his hands as if to show me. No wounds, nothing. His fire didn't even leave lasting marks on him. I put my hands in his without thinking, and he squeezed mine tight. He was here. He was fine. Things were...not fine, but at least he was. That's all that mattered for now.

"You're okay."

"Yeah."

"How'd it go? Are you hurt? How many were there? I couldn't tell because that one felt so intense!"

Ava looked at Kaiden, an impatient glare forming on his face. "There were three. One greater demon, and two lesser demons."

What were they talking about? Greater demon? Lesser demon?

"A greater demon? Is that one of the big ones? Oh, man! That must be why it felt so different! That thing felt damn scary, didn't it?"

I stared back and forth between them. "Wait, you can feel the difference between certain demons?"

"Yeah," Ava said. "Well, Kaiden can. I'm still trying to learn."

"You should have seen him sensing the big one! He like, doubled over! Your boyfriend is too cute when he's trying too hard!"

I whirled around to face Kaiden, eyebrows crinkling into a death glare. Kaiden shuddered, but his grin remained in place. As if everything was fine, when it so obviously was not fine.

It was the last straw for me. Everything was fun and games to him. Maybe because he suffered no consequences for his actions. Instead, Ava and I were left to deal with the fallout of Kaiden's recklessness.

"This isn't funny, Kaiden. This isn't a game. Ava could have been hurt, or worse, you know."

"I know that. But he didn't. He's fine." Kaiden gestured his hand to Ava. "See? All in one piece."

"Chay, I'm fine. Really. It's okay."

Ava's hand clasped my shoulder, but that did nothing to calm me down. I was already too far gone in my rage. I shrugged his hand off me, stepping closer to Kaiden. "That's not the point. Don't you care how dangerous that was for him?" I asked Kaiden.

"Of course I care." Kaiden looked crestfallen for a moment, biting his lip. Then, he stared back at me, defiance in his eyes. "But don't you think he can take care of himself? He *does* have superpowers, you know." So did I. But Ava was still just flesh and bone, a person.

"That doesn't mean he's invincible, Kaiden."

Kaiden scoffed. "Damn well near it."

"I'm glad you think so highly of me," Ava chimed in.

Kaiden waved a hand dismissively. "Bah, they're no match for you."

I gritted my teeth and grabbed at Kaiden's shirt. "This is all your fault, you know. You need to take some damn responsibility for this. I'm so tired of you making everything worse!"

"What do you mean, worse? I was only trying to help!"

"Chay, what's gotten into you?" Ava touched my shoulder and pulled me back from Kaiden. "Enough, from both of you. He's right. I'm not invincible, Kaiden. And now more demons could come."

Kaiden's eyes grow wide with disbelief. "Ava..." His face fell, and he glanced down as Ava pulled me into his arms.

"Just breathe, Chay. Deep and slow. Breathe."

His hands rubbed soothingly up and down my back, and despite myself, I did as he said, breathing in slowly, then exhaling. Dy used to do this for me. I felt my body relax. I nudged my forehead into his neck.

"I was just so worried about you." I bit my lip, fighting

back the sob that wanted to come out.

Ava kissed my cheek and held me closer. I was sure he could feel me shaking now. "It's okay."

For now.

It was only okay for now. What about the next time, and the next time, and the next? When would this end? Would it ever end? I didn't want this to continue. There had to be something I could do.

"Can I stay?" I pulled back to look at him hopefully.

"You know Kaiden's staying here while he recovers from the concussion, right? You still want to stay?"

I wasn't ready to let go of him yet. I didn't want to be alone—alone with my thoughts, alone after all that had happened today. Kaiden being here, though, was probably awful for my mental state. When I glanced his direction again, he was perched on the spare bed with his hands tucked under his legs, chewing on his lip and looking miles away. Probably because I'd just yelled at him.

I shook off the wave of guilt and returned my gaze to Ava. "I don't want to leave you."

"Okay, well. He never shuts up. You've been warned." Ava held me closer.

Ava pulled me to his bed and settled in with me. Kaiden flopped over and faced the wall, not looking at us. Seemed like we wouldn't have to worry about him gabbing all night long after all. Good.

"Think you were a bit hard on him?" Ava whispered.

Not really, no, I wanted to say. I held back that reply and simply shrugged. For all that Kaiden had put us through, he deserved to get a stern talking to. He had to learn that his choices didn't always affect just him.

"What happened with your cousins?" Ava asked.

I turned in his arms and curled my fingers into his shirt,

burying my face in his sweet and spicy smelling hair. "Let's talk about it tomorrow," I whispered back. This wasn't a conversation I wanted to have around Kaiden, even if he was currently petrified.

Right now, all I wanted was to stay close to Ava, and never let go.

CHAPTER NINE

AVARI

THE DRAB VOICES of the morning news jolted me from my sleep. I groaned and rubbed my eyes. Kaiden was sitting up on the other bed, hunched over and staring at the TV with a distant look on his face. He was totally spaced out. I closed my eyes again.

I had other things I was more concerned with, or rather, people. Chay was in my arms, and had slept there all night. He didn't usually stay. His face nuzzled into the crook of my neck, and his hands moved down my chest.

"Is it morning already?" He whispered in my ear, giving me goosebumps.

I nodded, and he sighed, burying his face further into me. My lips curled up a fraction when he inhaled, breathing in my scent.

"Hey, when are you guys gonna get up?" Kaiden blurted, shattering the moment and forcing me back to reality, which I didn't want to face. Damn it, Kaiden. Why was he always the one to interrupt and ruin everything?

I growled and bent my head up a fraction. "We're up," I muttered.

Chay and I sat up and I stretched my arms over my head. Kaiden smiled only slightly, rather than the beaming grin that seemed so natural on him. Chay was bordering on frowning, and wasn't looking at Kaiden.

"Yay!" Kaiden exclaimed. "What's the battle plan for today?"

"You're staying here," I said as I stood and smoothed out my bed-wrinkled black tee. "The adults need to go have a talk."

"Aw, what?" Kaiden pouted. "That's low, man."

I shrugged, unmoved by his sudden moroseness. "Just stay here while we go have a talk. We can get breakfast when we come back."

"Yeah, yeah." Kaiden waved me off and flopped down on the bed with his hands locked behind his head. "I got it. The kid'll stay here where he's outta trouble."

Man, he was being a bit of a downer, wasn't he? Still bothered by Chay's outburst, if I had to guess.

"Where do you want to go?" I asked.

"Somewhere far away," Chay said, his voice distant and full of longing. I had the sense that he didn't just mean that in the literal sense.

"Would you like to go flying?"

His head shot up. "Do you think that's safe?"

I shrugged. "Safe as it can be. We don't have to go very far, and if anything did happen, I'd protect you."

"Ava..."

I touched his cheek. "I have to protect you. I can't just...not. So let me, okay? Let me take care of you."

Chay put his hand over mine, and nodded.

We walked hand in hand the rest of the way to the cover of the trees, and took off once we were shrouded by the leaves, him touching his earring and sprouting wings from nowhere, while I had to remove my shirt, as usual. It'd be so convenient if mine worked that way. They did completely conceal themselves once they folded inward, leaving my back looking as normal—well, as normal as it could except for two thin raised lines, and the scars from scratch marks left behind when I was younger and my wings were coming in. To be able to just materialize them would be a blessing. Mine were just a curse. How fitting was that? Chay and I really were a pair, weren't we? A blessing and a curse, a light and darkness, a hero and a villain.

I was worried the whole time we were in the air that we'd run into more demons. I kept my eyes and my mind peeled for any disturbances, hoping maybe I'd pick up on something, even though I was still abysmal at this. We landed, and Chay's wings disappeared as he sank down on the rooftop. He let out a heavy sigh. His head was down, and he looked utterly dejected. I kneeled down in front of him.

"So, what did your cousin say?"

"He said he wanted me to come back home."

"What?" My eyes widened. Fear planted seeds in my chest, and my heart clenched. "You're not going to, are you?" I wouldn't just let him go. Not after all that we'd already been through. I kneeled in front of him and grabbed onto his shoulders.

"I don't plan on it." Chay put his hands on my shoulders, too, and we held on like we were each other's anchor. Maybe we were.

"Okay. Good." I kissed his hair. "But why does he want you to leave?"

Chay grimaced. "He knows about me being Falcon, Ava. I'm not sure how, but he knows. I...kinda panicked and ran off after he started talking about taking me home."

"What? How?"

Chay sighed. "I don't know. But he knows about my earrings, and that Chala gave them me. He wasn't making much sense. He said something about us doing what Chala wished of us. I freaked out after that and bailed. I feel awful for doing that, but I was just... It was overwhelming, and I got anxious."

"Hey, it's okay." I rubbed his arms and pulled him closer. "I get it. I get overwhelmed sometimes, too." I hadn't expected this. For one, I hadn't even known Chay had cousins, ones that seemed close at that. We hadn't exactly talked much about family, outside of him telling me his parents had died when he was young, and Chala looked after him. After I told him I was an orphan, we'd just kinda left it at that. Maybe he hadn't wanted to bring it up so he wouldn't hurt my feelings, since I didn't have any family.

"No, Ava, it's— " Chay worried his lip and averted his eyes. "It's different. I... I used to get anxious and down in the dumps, like, a lot."

"What do you mean?" Everyone got like that sometimes. Right? That was just part of life. And it wasn't like either of us had the best experience as kids.

"Ava, I..." He took a breath and met my gaze. "I have anxiety and depression. I have since I was young, since I lost my parents."

"Oh," I blurted. I wasn't sure what else to say to that, and now I felt like an awful person for never realizing. Chay was always so together, Chay was...perfect. "I, uh. I didn't know that." I was stumbling, making this worse. Gah, I sucked at this.

"It's okay. I was managing myself really well, until recently. You couldn't have known."

I didn't miss the way he said *was*. So, he wasn't managing well anymore. Something had happened to throw him off, and I didn't need three guesses what. It was me, and the shit he'd gone through for me recently. Shit. I really was no good for him, wasn't I? Golden boy was doing great before I came along and fucked him back up with my mayhem and villainy and demons, wasn't he? I exhaled and stood back up, turning away from him.

"Ava, it's okay, really. Sorry, this isn't what we came to talk about."

Right. We were supposed to be talking about Dyami, Chay's asshole cousin, not how I'd traumatized my boyfriend and triggered his anxiety. Chay stepped up behind me, and he placed a hand on my shoulder, lightly, gently.

"Turn around?" He asked me. I took a long breath and complied.

"So, your cousin. He knows, and wants you to leave."

"Yeah. But I don't want to, obviously."

I already didn't like this guy. Barging in here, telling Chay what to do and how he wasn't using his powers as intended. Who was he to say that? So what if he was Chay's cousin?

"Did he say anything else?"

Chay bit his lip and looked hesitant. "He...said you were dangerous."

Oh, was that how it was? I was the bad guy? Corrupting his poor, innocent cousin? This guy really was something. Was he wrong, though? "Well, I am dangerous," I admitted. After all, it wasn't a lie. I was.

"Not to me, though. He seemed to think I was in grave danger around you."

Well. Not like I could say that wasn't true, either. What had I managed to do thus far, except get into trouble and hurt Chay? I *was* a grave danger to him. Danger was practically my middle name. Or destruction. Both followed me everywhere I went, an endless cycle.

"Ava...you're not dangerous."

My lips turned downwards. "I have a hard time believing that. Look at the mess I've made."

"You haven't. You're not to blame here."

I turned away from him, balling my fists. "But I am. All I've done is make your life hell since the day we met."

Why would Chay ever want to put up with me? I was a horrible, selfish person. When he first approached me, I'd been awful to him, rude and snarky and abrasive. Why would he want me? I wasn't good for him. I'd already tried to shut him out, and leave him, and I'd backpedaled, why? Because of love? Yeah, right. Love. When had I turned into such a sap?

"You're wrong, Ava." He walked around in front of me, grabbed one of my fists, and put it to his heart. Automatically, I splayed my hand there, unable to help myself. We locked eyes. "I love you. I would do anything for you."

"I don't understand why."

"You don't choose who you love." His other hand reached out to touch my cheek, feather light. Even now, he restrained himself around me, careful not to push me to my limits. I didn't deserve his overwhelming kindness and generosity, and I wasn't sure I ever would. "Don't beat yourself up over any of this. Okay? Don't do this again."

Those captivating midnight eyes held me, pleading, begging. Did Chay know how easy it was for me to relent to him now? My heart was putty in his hands. I really had turned into a lovesick puppy.

"Okay," I said, placing a hand over his on my cheek, pressing his warm palm more firmly against my skin. Heaven. I exhaled and closed my eyes. "Has he tried to contact you since you ran off?"

"A few times. I haven't picked up or replied to his texts, though. I'm too scared to."

I pulled Chay closer. "It's okay." It was far from okay. Why were we an utter mess? Maybe if I assured him enough times, kept telling him it was okay, somehow, it would be. Or at the very least, it might help calm him down. If we were both messes, how would we hold it together?

We had enough issues as it was, and now this Dyami guy was wrecking Chay's emotions, telling him I was some menace, and for that, he was already my enemy. How dare he do this to Chay. How dare he presume to tell him what he did with his power was wrong. It was Chay's gift, and he could do what he wanted with it.

"Why does he think he gets to have a say in what the hell you do with your life, and powers, anyway?" I blurted.

"Well... After Chala was gone, he was the one that was there for me. In a way, he's the closest living person I have to a parent. He's the one who helped me learn to manage my mental illness, and helped me with my homework, and college applications. The only reason I'm even here is because of his help." Chay tightened his hold on me, body quaking. He held back a sob. "That's why... I don't understand. I worked so hard to be something more, and to leave the rez and come here. And now, it feels like it's all falling apart. Like—like I'm falling apart."

"Shh, it's okay," I said, rubbing his back more. I had to hold it together. For Chay. If I wasn't calm and collected, if I wasn't there for him...would he descend further into despair? I didn't want that. This troubled, melancholy version of Chay made me uneasy. Maybe this was the real Chay. The smiling, sunshine boy was a carefully cultivated mask he wore to make it look like he was a perfectly functional person on the outside. I'd shattered that mask, blown open the doors, and thrown his world back into chaos. Hadn't I?

"I'm not leaving. I won't."

I didn't want to let him go either, despite myself, despite only wrecking things more by keeping him close to me. I wasn't letting Chay go ever again. Was that selfish of me?

CHAYTON

I HELD ONTO Ava for what could've been minutes or hours, never wanting to let go of him.

He knows now. He knows.

I hadn't set out this morning to tell him about my mental illness. It'd just sort of happened. I only wanted to explain about Dy. All I'd done was make things worse, probably.

I wanted to melt away in Ava's arms. I wanted nothing more than to slink back into bed, preferably with Ava and without Kaiden, and just be a cocoon until all my problems went away. Of course, that wouldn't work. But I still wanted it. Even just a few minutes of peace. That probably wasn't going to happen any time soon.

The longer I held onto Ava, the more anxious I grew. He was still a bit stiff, only relaxed a fraction, and I suspected it was because of everything I'd just told him. I pulled back so I could look at him, but kept my arms at his sides.

"I guess I'm going to have to talk to him," I said, and sighed.

Ava scowled and held me tighter, wings bristling behind him. "I don't like this. Let me come with you."

"No, it's probably better if I go alone. Based on what he's said already, I don't think it's a good idea for you to be there." Ava's scowl only deepened as I went on. I touched his cheek and his face softened, just a little, revealing that kind, soft on the inside Ava that only I knew. "It'll be okay. I'm not going anywhere, regardless of what he says. Okay?"

He wasn't the only one I needed to convince that things would be okay. I wasn't sure things would ever be okay. But that was nothing new. I just had to push through, keep pushing through, like I had all this time. Eventually, the nagging voices in my head would quiet down, if I distracted myself enough, if I pushed back enough.

"I still think it's a bad idea," he said.

"Wouldn't you want to know if someone knew more about your past?"

There was a conflict running through his face, an indecision. He'd been through the same thing with his dad, and I was terrified for him the whole time. This wasn't much different. The only difference was talking with Dy wasn't dangerous, while Ava had stirred up demons to get to his dad.

"Yeah, I would." He leaned his head against mine and sighed. "You promise, nothing he says will change how you feel? I get the feeling he doesn't like me."

"Never."

Ava was my everything, and I wasn't going to give him up so easily. I'd fought tooth and nail to keep him here with me, and I wasn't about to just leave him after that.

I pulled my phone out of my pocket and checked it. Three more missed calls from Dy. I took a deep breath and texted him.

I'm ready to talk now.

"I guess we can head back while I wait for him to reply or call me again."

"Okay."

I brought my wings back out and we soared into the air. Every so often, Ava glanced at me as we flew back, mouth agape like he wanted to say something, but he didn't.

We were about halfway back when Ava suddenly veered downward and alofted on a nearby building to yank out his phone. He pressed the screen forcefully with a grunt and put it up to his ear. I landed beside him, eyeing him with concern.

"What? Why have you called like six times?" Ava's eyes widened. "What?! How many?" His eyes squinted together, as if he was straining to concentrate. Tinny yapping was coming from his phone, and I could tell it was Kaiden's voice on the line, but couldn't make out his words. "Yeah, yeah. I feel them."

"What?" I asked, my stomach already in knots. I had a hunch what the answer would be, but I didn't want to be right.

"More demons are coming."

Terror seized my veins, making them go cold. My throat tightened as if an icy hand had wrapped around it. "Wh-where?" More importantly, why were there more? Why now, and why did they just keep coming for Ava?

"Heading right for us."

No. Not right now. This couldn't be happening right now.

"Let's hurry before they catch up," I said.

"They'll just follow us." Ava sighed and dragged a hand through his unkempt hair, then looked at me with resolve in his eyes. "I'll go take care of them."

My heart raced wildly at that, my chest tight with a bubble of anxiety. "N-No! You can't, Ava!" I grabbed one of his hands with both of mine and held it tight, as if that could keep him from leaving.

"Chay..." His resolve appeared to wither, only a little. He shook his head. "I have to. They'll just come after me, and if we run, we'll be leading them right to our doorstep."

"There has to be some other way!" I held his hand tighter, pleading with everything I had and hoping it would come through. He averted his eyes, lips turning downward. I couldn't take this. My anxiety couldn't take this. My insides were a jumble right now. I might vomit. "I-I can't take it, Ava."

"I'm sorry." His other hand came up to caress my cheek. Normally, that would have comforted me. Now, all I could feel was anguish as he looked into my eyes. "I have to. I'll protect you, no matter what."

A chasm tore open in my chest. There was no stopping him, was there? No stopping this. How could he be so calm, so determined? He faced danger like it was nothing, like he was an untamable, indestructible force. In comparison to me, he was.

I looked down. He stepped back from me, taking his hand from mine. The chasm widened, engulfing my lungs, making it hard to breathe.

"Hide somewhere safe," he said, and I couldn't form a

reply, robbed of my breaths in my rising panic. All I could do was watch as he took off, flying head first into the face of danger.

I wanted to go after him, but my fear and panic petrified me. I sunk down and held my knees to my chest. Tears burned my eyes and it felt like a hand was closed around my throat. When I tried to breathe, it just gripped harder. I sandwiched my head between my knees and tried to remember to breathe slower and deeper.

Everything is okay. Everything will be okay. Deep, slow breaths. In and out. In and out. Calm.

I repeated my mantras, but they did nothing. The moment I stopped, my breaths quickened and my panic rose again.

I was so useless. I couldn't do anything to help Ava. I couldn't fight because I couldn't even see what he was fighting. I couldn't protect him. Instead, I was left to sit here while he went off to protect me. All I could do was hope he'd come back to me safe.

"Chay?"

I jumped at the familiar and soft, concerned voice. When I looked up, I saw...Ona?

At least, I thought it was Ona. Those big doe eyes were unmistakable behind the feathered mask that resembled an owl.

"Is that you, Ona?" How had he even gotten up here? Climbed? Why was he here, anyways?

"Yeah." He smiled and stepped over, kneeling down to look at me. "What's wrong? Why have you been crying?"

I wiped my eyes and sniffed. "It's nothing." I couldn't say anything about Ava. Not to Ona, not to anyone.

He offered his hand and I took it, letting him pull me up. I rubbed at my blurry eyes and focused on him, gasping when my vision had cleared.

Ona had a set of wings.

AVARI

WE JUST HAD a little more to go before we got back to campus, when some demons reared their ugly heads. Why couldn't they buzz off?

I flew towards the dark, sinister feeling, palms sweating and fingers trembling.

I pulled my mask out of my pocket and slipped it on. Chay wouldn't be pleased I'd started carrying it around with me again, but it was necessary if demons could come after me at any given moment.

It felt like another one of greater demons. Damn. More and more of those were showing up.

I could really use someone like my dad to back me up right now. I wondered how far away he was now, and how many of the demons he had even lured away from this area, because there sure as hell still seemed to be a lot. They were moths, and I the flame.

My dad being in close proximity probably would have made things worse. Still, that didn't make being stuck doing this on my own feel any better. I even would have taken Kaiden's help right now.

The bright red figure came into view, menacing with its massive wingspan. It sent goosebumps down my spine every time.

I steeled myself, taking a deep breath before zooming towards the beast, waiting until it saw me before suddenly veering upward, above the cover of the clouds to avoid unwanted onlookers.

I'm sure my last encounter had riled up a bunch more demons in the area. At this rate, I'd never be free of them. I'd be stuck fighting them eternally, because they just kept coming. Is that what it was like for my dad? I felt like I was fighting a losing battle. Fight the demons, attract more, repeat.

I wasn't helping my dad by continuing to fight them. But I had no other choice when they kept showing up on my figurative doorstep. *I'm sorry, Dad. Wherever you are, I hope you're okay*.

Time to fry some demons.

CHAPTER TEN

CHAYTON

I STARED AT Ona, unable to speak.

"Ona? What's going on? You...You have..." I couldn't finish my sentence.

"That's right. I have powers, too. Dy gave me this," Ona said, holding up a wrist and showing me a braided bracelet with a carved feather charm. "And it gives me superpowers! Oh, and I'm supposed to go by Owl while I'm like this. It's like, my code name. He pronouns today by the way. Dy insists I put my pin in my pocket while we're out in our masks."

What was going on right now?

I made a few false starts before I could compose myself and say anything else. "Dy gave you that?"

"Yep! He has one, too. His is a necklace. And Tah has a ring!"

All of them had powers? I stared at him in disbelief. Why had Dy never said anything to me? Was it because he didn't know Chala had given me something, too?

"All of you? Why?" Had Chala done all this on purpose? And what for? Suddenly, I was questioning what Chala really wanted me to do with these powers. She'd given Dy and Tah items, as well as another to Dy for later? Furthermore, he gave it to Ona, who was younger than me and came from outside our reservation?

"Oh! I've probably said too much!" Owl gave me a sheepish grin and slapped a hand over his mouth. "It's probably better if Dy tells you everything."

All of this was so sudden. My stomach flipped at the thought of talking to Dy. I had to, though. It was time to learn the truth.

"Okay."

"Let's go!"

Owl took to the air before I could object. Ava was out there, fighting the demons. I should've waited for him to come back, but Owl was already on his way without me. I flew after him.

I wasn't even sure which way Ava had gone. I pulled out my phone and texted him, so at least maybe he'd see it later.

I'm going to talk to Dy. Please make it back to me safe, Ava. I love you.

My body trembled with fear, and my heart ached with worry. If I had Ava with me, this might've been easier. I couldn't turn back now. I needed to find out the answers.

A loud boom tore through the air. I jumped and almost dropped my phone. I shoved it into my pocket and nearly bumped into Owl, who was stopped dead in the air.

"Whoa! What was that?" He pointed to a huge puff of smoke rising from nearby.

Oh no. My stomach roiled.

"Ava..."

AVARI

THE THING WAS so damn slow, following me at a snail's pace. It was almost whale-like, floating along in the ocean of clouds, somewhat despondent, somewhat interested, at least I assumed, since it kept following me. Staying out of the thing's reach was pretty damn easy. For now.

As long as it didn't decide there was something more interesting than me and stopped following me. All I cared about was keeping it away from Chay. I doubted it would just turn tail and go after him, though. To demons, I was like a bug zapper, a bright beacon that they were drawn to. Except, if they got too close, I had no choice but to zap them.

The demon let out a low growl that practically made the whole sky rumble. It started shooting towards me at an alarming speed for its size, which I learned from past experience was not to be underestimated. I sped up and kept one eye on it. But it was faster.

Before I could get out of the way, the demon pummeled into me and batted me down with a whoosh of its wings, sending me back through the clouds. As soon as I pulled myself back together, I popped back through and looked around. Where the hell had it gone? The thing was huge, so there was no way I could miss it, yet it was nowhere to be found.

Something suddenly latched onto me from behind. Claws clutched into my skin. I was screwed. Where the hell had it come from?

The demon started a downward spiral, taking me down with it. I couldn't be taken down that easily. I simply *wouldn't* be taken down that easily. I refused. As long as I had fire power, I would fight back against these demon bastards. I grabbed onto the demon wherever I could get a hold, and I let my fire loose, not holding back. The demon wailed and let go just before it crashed down on the ground. I kept myself hovering just above it, panting for air.

"Take that, you damn demon!"

I threw a few balls of fire at it for good measure, forgetting myself in the (literal) heat of the moment. I was going to make sure this damn thing couldn't get back up. They could keep coming at me for as long as they wanted, but I refused to give up. Trails of smoke started rising from the demon's ashy corpse. It was only then, once the air was dense with demon ash that filled my lungs, that I stopped pummeling it with my fire.

"Ava!" When Chay called out, goosebumps shot down my spine. I'd gotten *far* too carried away.

I'd told him to hide. What the hell was he doing here? "Chay?"

I glanced around and spotted Chay, along with someone else, on top of a nearby parking garage. I swooped up and landed beside them.

"Chay, what are you doing here? And who is this?" I kept my distance, assessing this newcomer, with fluffy gray and white wings, and a feathered, owlish-looking bird mask on. Were there more winged people around playing superhero now?

"Hi, I'm On—Owl. He, him, and his pronouns today, please."

I stared, agape, not only at the way this guy introduced himself, but also still more than a little confused about what was happening here. I settled my gaze on Chay after a stunned moment looking back and forth between them. He met my eyes and offered a wan smile, brows raising apologetically.

"Apparently I'm not the only one who Chala gave powers to." Chay pointed to the person beside him. "That's Ona, and he told me Dy and Tah also have them."

There were others like Chay. He wasn't an original, one of a kind. This changed things, really changed things. Chay's whole damn family were superheroes now? What exactly had that Chala lady been trying to do, handing out superpowers like Halloween candy to kids?

"Hey, man. Don't go blabbing all our secrets to him!" Ona—Owl—said.

"It's okay," Chay said.

"What is going on right now?" I asked, still a bit flabbergasted by this whole situation, and now this Owl guy was talking about blabbing secrets like Chay was committing a sin

"I ran into him after you left. Actually, I texted you. I was going to go ahead and talk to Dy. I didn't think we'd run into you." Chay grimaced and clutched onto his braid, nibbling on his lip.

I gave him a watery smile. "I got carried away and made a mess of things." Apparently, that was all I was capable of. Making messes upon messes upon messes, and making new messes to clean up the old messes. I could do no right, only wrong.

"So, this is the guy, huh?" Owl tilted his head, and I half

expected it to keep on turning, like an actual Owl, but it didn't.

Oh, I was "the guy" now? Had Chay's cousins been talking about me? I thought of the death glare Dyami gave me, and wondered what it was he'd said to them. Could he tell what trouble I was just from one look? Was the word villain written that clearly on my forehead, or something? I was half tempted to wipe my forehead to check if marker rubbed off on my hand.

"Um..." Chay worried his lip more and looked at me cautiously.

Owl took a step forward, surveying me and I automatically took one back. "This dude doesn't look that dangerous to me."

I raised a brow. Dangerous, was I? He started circling around me, making me feel like I was being hunted by a bird of prey. "Excuse you," I blurted, stepping out of his circular path.

"Oh, are you not okay with the terms dude and guy? What are your pronouns?" Owl turned his head to the side again, looking at me curiously.

I gave him an incredulous look. He'd completely mistook what I was offended about. "Those terms are fine. I use he and him pronouns..." No one had ever asked me that before. I tried not to assume about anyone myself, though. "What do you want with Chay?"

"Sorry, dude, but I really shouldn't say anything." Owl put his hands up as if to surrender, or convince me not to hurl fireballs at his face (though if I did that, I'd have a lot of explaining to do). He gave me a sheepish grin, showing his teeth off. "I don't want any trouble, man."

"I'm trouble, am I?" I crossed my arms and hardened my stare.

"Owl, stop." Chay stepped between us, putting a hand out to keep us from each other's throats. "He's not trouble. I trust him, okay? It's fine." Chay looked back at Owl, while Owl's eyes darted between us as if conflicted, trying to put pieces together, although he lacked all the pieces to do so. Even so, he nodded at Chay and gave me a tenuous smile.

"Well, if you say so..."

"I do." Chay stepped by my side.

"Hm." Owl cocked his head again and put a hand to his chin. "So, like, what's your deal, then?"

Like I would tell him all that so easily. I eyed him suspiciously. Before I could answer that, something slammed into my back, knocking me down and pinning me.

"Get away from him!" The person holding me down shouted.

CHAYTON

DY—WHO I recognized from his gray streaked hair—swooped in out of nowhere and tackled Raven to the ground, yelling "Get away from him!"

"Dy? What are you doing?" I stepped towards him where he had Raven held down on his belly like he was making a citizen's arrest.

There was another swoop, and someone landed beside me, grabbing my arm. I glanced over at a person with a red and brown feathered mask, and a familiar undercut.

"Tah?" I stared in disbelief. Why were they all here now? What was happening?

"We need to get Chay away from him! Owl, Hawk, grab Chay!"

"Got it!" Owl said, coming to my other side and taking hold of the opposite arm Tah had.

"What are you doing?" I tried to pull out of their grasps, but both of them held on tighter.

"We're getting you away from this monster," Dy said, holding onto Raven's shoulders. Raven tried to wriggle around, to spread his hands out, but when flames started to form in his hands, some unseen force seemed to extinguish them.

"What are you talking about? He isn't a monster! Dy!"

Tah—Dy had called him Hawk—and Owl pulled me further back, away from Dy and Raven. My heart lodged in my throat. I didn't understand what was happening. Why was he doing this?

"I'm sorry, Chay. It's going to be okay," Hawk whispered as he held both my arms while Owl touched my earring. My wings, along with all my strength and speed, vanished. Hawk's assurance felt empty. Things didn't feel like they would be okay at all. That bottomless pit was opening beneath my feet again, and my own family was dragging me down into the depths. Betrayal and confusion and despair all roiled in my stomach, along with my anxiety, making me nauseous.

"No! What are you doing? Stop!" I struggled in Hawk's grip, but it was useless without my Falcon strength. Hawk lifted me up and started flying away from Dy and Raven. "Please don't do this. You've got to take me back." I wriggled, against Hawk, and inwardly against my mounting helplessness and looming, anxious depression. *They can't do this. They just can't.* But they were. And there was nothing I could do.

"I'm sorry, Chay. I can't do that."

I struggled helplessly, while Dy and Raven were struggling below, fading from my view.

"Why not?"

"It's going to be okay. We won't let anything happen to you now."

What did he mean by that? Why did they all act like they had to *save* me from something? Or someone... I fell limp against his chest and held in a sob. I didn't try to stop the cloud of depression from raining down on me any more.

CHAPTER ELEVEN

AVARI

"LET GO OF me, you damn asshole!"

I scrabbled and fought with Dyami, but every time I tried to muster up some fire, a gust of air whooshed over my palms and blew it out. I had no clue what the hell was going on with that, but it was annoying as hell. He had me pinned on my front, so I couldn't even see the damn bastard.

"Now, you listen here. I know what you are," he seethed into my ear, making the hairs on the back of my neck stand on end. I wanted him *off* of me. I struggled more, growling. How dare he restrain me and put his hands on me.

"Do you?"

"You're a monster."

Hmph. Like I hadn't heard that one before. Freak,

monster, problem child, weirdo... You name it. Why did *he* think that, though? What had I done to make him so damn angry?

"What's it to you? Why do you give a damn what I am?"

"Because I'm not going to let you hurt Chay."

What the hell was even talking about? I would *never* hurt Chay. What demented logic was running through his head to make him think this? I threw all my weight into my efforts now, managing to heft him off of me and roll over.

"I have no intention of hurting Chay." I pushed myself up just in time for him to dive at me again, grabbing my wrists and pinning them at my sides. "You think you can just barge in here and put your damn hands on me? Get the hell off of me!" I wriggled more, made flames, only for more wind to breeze by and extinguish my palms yet again. Really, what the fresh hell was up with that? I growled.

"I don't believe a word you say, you monster!"

God damn, this guy was ten times more stubborn than Chay. Heat burned up my arms, and my vision practically went red.

"I'm *not* a monster!" I snarled at him. He was unphased by my pure rage, and damn it what was the deal with the wind gusts?

"You're the reason these monsters exist. You're no better than a demon."

I went wide-eyed. He knew about demons?

"How the hell do you know that?"

In my moment of shock, he let me go and rose into the air. Did he really think I was going to just let him leave?

"I'm going to make sure you can't hurt Chay. That's why I'm taking him home."

"The hell you are!"

Dyami looked down on me with such malice, with such

a stern and frightening glare—like I was a monster. I alighted to pursue him, and he had the nerve to turn *away* from me, as if I wasn't even a threat.

"Get back here!"

He spun around and raised his hand. A swift wind rushed over me and pushed me back down on top of the parking garage, knocking all the wind out of my lungs.

What the fuck?

CHAYTON

TAH TOOK US to a hotel and put me down in a chair. He and Ona sat on the beds, and Ona flipped on the TV.

"What's going on? Why did you guys take me here?"

"It's better if Dy explains everything. Just wait for him," Tah said. Ona started to open his mouth but Tah shushed him. "We wait for Dyami. Chay should hear it from him."

"But, Tah," Ona said, frowning.

"But, nothing. We wait for Dy."

So we waited. Ona flopped over and watched TV, Tah piddled on his phone, and I sat there with my gut churning, fighting back my stomach's urge to run to the bathroom and vomit.

It wasn't long, only a few minutes, before Dy came through the door.

"Dy!" I immediately blurted. "What the heck is going on?"

Dy's mouth was in a hard line. His face softened when

he saw me. He came up to me and kneeled down in front of the chair, staring up at me with the most intense, apologetic look I'd ever seen. I stared back at him in awe. He looked worse than I felt right now, like *he* was the one being put through this misery, not me.

"I'm sorry, Chay. I didn't know Chala had given you one of the gifts. I didn't know there was such great danger here. If I'd known what I was sending you into, I never would've put you through this." He put his hands on top of mine.

"Dy... What's going on? I—I don't understand. Why do you all have these powers, too?"

"Chay... Chala gave us this power to fight the demons."

Dy's words made me feel as if my whole world had been pulled out from under me, yet again. I couldn't believe what I was hearing. To fight demons? Red flashed across my vision. I was back above the Muir woods for a split second, a gaping, bloody hole in my chest. I squeezed my eyes shut. That wouldn't help, though. How could I fight those things? I couldn't even see them.

"H-How?"

His grip on my hands tightened. "Together, we can. We can teach you."

"But—But we can't see them. How can we?" I dared to open my eyes and look at him. He seemed... perplexed.

"What do you mean? You can't see them?"

"You can?"

"Well, yeah, we can see them!" Ona said, doing a hand to fist motion. "You really can't see the demons?"

"Ona," Dy barked, side eyeing him and shaking his head. He turned back to me and touched my cheek, leaning in to look at my earrings. "You should be able to. There must be something wrong with your earrings."

He brushed his thumb over my earlobe, but didn't

touch my earring. When Ona touched it, he'd been able to make my powers and wings go away, so I assumed Dy would be able to do the same. Nothing happened when Ava touched it, though. So strange. I took a couple deep breaths in an attempt to slow my breathing down. There was too much happening right now.

"I should?"

"Yes." He stroked my cheeks again, then took my hands, giving them a reassuring squeeze, only I wasn't reassured one bit. I was still waffling, drowning, wafting. "It's okay. We'll figure out why. It'll be okay." Words that once would've calmed me instantly did nothing for me now.

"Dy..."

"There's a lot more we need to talk about. Are you okay to keep talking?" He held my hands tighter, and I squeezed his back, bracing myself for the oncoming conversation.

I nodded meekly, even though I wasn't sure I was okay. It'd be more nerve wracking to put it off any longer.

"I never even suspected Chala had one last gift to give. She'd already entrusted the responsibilities of our line's gifts to me. I had an extra for the future, just in case."

"The extra's the one Dy gave to me!" Ona said, holding up his wrist with a pleased grin.

"I didn't even realize she'd given you one of the items, until I came to the city for a surprise visit, and on the news, I saw a mysterious superhero with brown wings. I'm so sorry I didn't know, Chay." He clasped my hands together in his and looked up at me, face torn with guilt. "I never wanted this for you. I wanted you to be able to find your own path, and do what made you happy."

I bit my lip and glanced at Ona and back to him. "That's why you chose Ona instead?"

He nodded. "After everything you've been through, I

didn't want to ask it of you. I knew it might be overwhelming at times for you." Dy sighed and looked down. "But it seems Chala made the decision for you instead. I know she only meant the best. I don't blame her. But I'm sorry."

Instead of a reply, I took a couple deep breaths and shook my head. I didn't want to know what he said next, but it was inevitable. I had to know why they had powers, too.

"Dy, it's not your fault." I pulled my hands from his and replaced them over his knuckles, giving him a weak smile.

"Thanks, coz."

"So... What do you do with the powers? You said you all can see the demons?"

Dy nodded.

"You bet we can!" Ona added. "We fight them!"

My eyes widened. "You really fight them?" Lika Ava? Only... "Can you sense them? Do they come after you?"

"We can sense them, but they can't sense us," Dy said.

"They can't see us coming and they don't know what hit 'em!" Ona added. "Right, Tah?"

"Yeah," Tah agreed, looking up from his phone. "They've got nothing on us." His mouth quirked up into a smirk.

They could fight them without the risk of it coming back to bite them. Ava only seemed to draw out more. If I could see them too...maybe I could protect Ava. I clutched a hand to my heart, chest pounding at the thought. As promising as it was, it was also frightening. I'd experienced first hand what those things were capable of. Could I really fight them?

"There's something else... or *someone*, we need to talk about, Chay."

My heart felt like it was in my throat. I swallowed

down a lump as my stomach dropped.

"Ava..."

"Do you realize what he is, Chay? Did he tell you?"

I clamped my eyes shut and looked away from him. Did *he* know? Should I tell him? How could I? Even if he suspected, I couldn't give away Ava's secrets like that.

"You do know." He touched my cheek and made me look at him again. "He's a Fallen One."

My eyes snapped open and I stared in shock at him. It was clear on my face now. There was no escaping it. So I whispered out, "Yes."

"I wonder if that's why you found him."

I gave him a skeptical, puzzled look. "What do you mean?"

"You must have felt his presence, something othering about him. Did you feel drawn to him? Like he stood out from all the rest?"

I managed a nod. My heart pounded in my ears. How did he know? I remembered the first time I saw Ava, and how different he felt. I watched him for a while before I ever spoke to him. It was only when we were paired up as lab partners that I finally found the courage to talk to him.

"Interesting. Even with his power in disarray, Chay was able to sense he was different," Tah noted with a hum of intrigue.

"The Fallen Ones are nothing but trouble, Chay," Dy continued. "We can sense the demons, and them, because they're no different. They're of the same ilk."

"What do you mean?"

"Did he tell you where demons come from, Chay?"

"No." I wanted to look away again. I wanted the void to open up under me and swallow me up, just so I wouldn't have to be here.

"Chay...The Fallen Ones turned into demons."

I shook my head and squeezed my eyes shut, trying to stop the sting of tears. "No."

Dy touched my cheek. I jerked away from him. "That boyfriend of yours is just one step away from becoming a monster. The Fallen Ones are doomed to turn into demons."

"No, no." I stood and held onto my head. I couldn't control my breathing now. My knees wobbled. Why? Why hadn't Ava ever told me this?

Hot tears slid down my cheeks. Dy caught me before I could fall to the floor. No matter how many times I sobbed out the word no, no matter how much I shook my head, it didn't change what Dy had just told me. I didn't want to believe it. There was no way that Ava, *my* Ava, could turn into one of those things that came after him, that hurt me... Was there?

Was Ava doomed to turn into a monster?

CHAPTER TWELVE

AVARI

BY THE TIME I was able to get back up, Dyami was long gone. Damn, and I thought Chay was fast. They'd taken Chay. Where to, I had no freaking clue.

What the hell was going on? How did Dyami know about the demons anyways?

He seemed to think I was no different than one of those monsters. I wasn't like them, though. The demons I fought were lesser and greater demons, or as Kaiden I sometimes fondly called them, small fries and big ones. Even if I were to commit the atrocities that would result in my turning into a demon, feeding on human souls, I wouldn't turn into a mindless monster.

At least, as far as I was aware. My dad hadn't talked

about the Fallen who were now demons much. I wondered now where they were, what they were called, and why the hell they created so many damn demons. If I ever met one, I'd kick those big shots' asses.

How much exactly did Dyami know? More importantly, did Chay know? If he didn't, chances were, Dyami was telling all now. Not explaining all the fine details about the demons to Chay now seemed like a mistake that I would pay dearly for.

I ruminated more on that, kicking myself inwardly as I flew back to campus. A demon could have come to bite me at that moment, and I wouldn't have cared. Demons be damned back to hell where they belonged. I couldn't have mustered the effort to blow their asses up.

Chay was gone. I had no idea where they took him. Once Dyami got in his head with all these notions of how I was some awful monster out to steal his soul, he might not come back.

I walked through the campus in a numb haze, barely registering the movement of my feet, barely conscious of anything but the absence of Chay and enough to avoid running into people. When I got to my door, I took a deep breath. Now I had to deal with Kaiden's hyper ass, and explain why Chay hadn't come back from our talk.

That wouldn't be easy. I couldn't just say "oh yeah, Chay's family flew off with him, and by the way, Chay is Falcon and turns out his family all have the same powers". Oh, he'd just eat that up. I couldn't say a damn thing. It'd be easier if I could.

"Ava!" Kaiden launched himself at me, almost tackling me, but having the forethought to stop short with his hands half outstretched, not touching me. The consideration for my personal space gave me little satisfaction, though.

I'd half hoped he would've up and left while we were gone. Of course, I wouldn't be so lucky. Bad luck seemed to be in over-abundance these days. Well, whatever.

"Hey," I mumbled, then schlepped over to my bed and flopped down on it. I was in no mood to do anything else, not even go get breakfast. The morning's events had killed any appetite I could've possibly had.

"Ava! What's going on? What's wrong?" He held a finger out. I slapped his hand away before the offending finger could touch me.

"Stop it. Go home, Kaiden." I turned on my side to face the wall.

"Why? What happened? Where's Chay? Did you guys get in a fight or something?"

"I don't want to talk about it. Just go."

Just thinking about it was making my eyes sting. I had no idea what to do now, no clue if Chay would come back. That thought alone stabbed at my chest, made my throat tighten, and my eyes burn.

"Come on, man. You can talk to me."

Could I, really? I mean, I could tell Kaiden *some* things. Not this, though. I couldn't trust him with this.

I shot up and glared at him. Maybe, if I were firm enough, he'd go away before I became a total mess. "Chay is gone." My eyes stung. I felt a tear slide down my cheek. Damn it. So much for firm. That wasn't what I even wanted to say.

"What do you mean, gone?"

I wiped my eyes. "Th-they took him."

"Who took him? Was it demons? I thought I felt some! Did they hurt him?" Kaiden gasped and covered his mouth. "Is... Is he...?"

"No. God, no. He's alive. It wasn't the demons. I took care

of those. It was his cousins."

"Oh." Kaiden exhaled. "Well, that's a relief," he said, then looked at me, perplexed. "But wait, why are you so upset then? What's the big deal? He's coming back, isn't he?"

"I... I don't know." I swallowed and choked on a sob. The tears pricking at my eyes broke free against my wishes.

Kaiden reached a hand out and touched the top of my head. "Ava..." That only made it worse. My tears turned to full on ugly crying, which was the last thing I wanted to be doing in front of Kaiden. Damn it, they wouldn't stop now that they'd started. Kaiden pulled me against him, and I didn't have it in me to stop him. I sobbed against his shirt until my tear ducts felt dry.

I WOKE UP and rubbed my eyes, which were crusty with dried tears. My head hurt like hell. Had I passed out after balling my eyes out? In front of Kaiden. Kaiden... I groaned and focused my eyes, and that was when I saw Kaiden's face right in front of mine.

He slept in bed with me?!

I shot up, chest heaving in panic. We were both still fully clothed. Phew.

I mean, I didn't think I was *that* vulnerable. I didn't think I'd do that with Kaiden, even at my most vulnerable. Even as grating and teasing as Kaiden was, I liked to think we had an understanding, and that his teasing was just that—a tease, and not something he'd ever act on unless I expressed clear interest, which I hadn't. That probably wouldn't even happen if I were inebriated.

I thought back to earlier, when he pulled me into his

arms and just let me cry. He was uncharacteristically quiet, for once. He let me cry until I couldn't anymore, and then he pushed me down on the bed and told me to just get some sleep. I protested when he lay down right in front of me. He said to just relax, and we'd figure out what to do when I calmed down.

I was tired and beaten down, so I didn't fight it anymore, and let myself drift off. And now, here I was. Did he have to stay in my bed, though?

Kaiden sat up and stretched, yawning loudly.

"Hey," he said sleepily. "Feel any better?"

"No. Why did you sleep in my bed?"

Kaiden shrugged. "I didn't feel right leaving you alone."

"There's two beds in my room, you know."

Kaiden grinned sheepishly. "Yeah, but...you needed comforting."

I rolled my eyes and pushed him off my bed. "Personal space doesn't go out the window just because I cried my eyes out in front of you."

"Hey! Ouch!" Kaiden stared up at me, bottom lip pushed out.

"Serves you right," I grumbled. I didn't care. In fact, I didn't care about anything right now. If Chay didn't come back... What would I do?

I yanked my phone out of my pocket. No missed calls or texts from him. Should I try to call? I'd been out for a couple of hours. Maybe they were still talking. Talking about me, about how bad I was for Chay. Were they wrong, though?

"We should go get breakfast!" Kaiden said from the floor, springing up to his feet.

"I'm not hungry." Conveniently, my stomach gurgled in protest.

"That belly of yours says otherwise!" Kaiden snickered.

"Come on. My treat, one Avari special, no strings attached."

"No strings attached?" I raised an eyebrow at him. "You're not gonna hassle me for all the juicy details like you usually do?" Color me surprised. Kaiden, not playing the interrogator for once? Tempting offer.

"Not over breakfast." Kaiden winked with a crooked grin.

Of course. There was always a catch. I rolled my eyes at him. That was better than him pressing me in the middle of breakfast, where other people might overhear us. "Fine, fine. I guess that's as good as I'll get from you."

Free waffles would normally be far more appealing. Even my glorious Oreo topped breakfast dessert couldn't drag me out of the hold of wallowing self-pity I was currently slipping further down into by the second.

"Yay! One Avari special, coming up!"

With the promise of waffles in mind, I maundered along beside Kaiden to our destination. He babbled the whole way of course, while I wallowed and brooded and barely listened. I half-heartedly poked at my waffles while we ate, and tried to actually listen to some of what Kaiden was saying for once.

Kaiden could carry on a conversation with a rock, which I might as well have been to him most of the time, for all that I paid attention. His incessant chattering was, for once, a welcome distraction from the thoughts that plagued me and the uneasy knot in my belly that made it hard to eat. I rested my chin in my palm as I prodded at my waffle. Right now he was talking about if Oreos were better with regular or chocolate milk.

"Impossible choice," I interjected.

Kaiden stared at me like I had three eyes. "Are you okay? Or are you interested in the conversation because it's about

Oreos?"

"No, and no."

Kaiden gawked and blinked as he took in my answer. Before he could say anything else, I stood and dumped my half-eaten waffle, leaving Kaiden to scramble and holler "Wait up!" as he hurried to follow.

"So, when are you gonna tell me what actually happened?" Kaiden asked when he caught up with me. He couldn't even last ten seconds after we finished our breakfast to start back in with this crap.

"Chay's cousins took him," I said dully, though on the inside I felt anything but.

"Took him? As in, like, forced him to go?"

"Yeah, something like that." Easier than telling him they literally picked him up and flew away.

"That's it? What did they say? How come you didn't stop them?"

"I couldn't." I sighed and picked up my pace, wanting nothing more than to go back to my room and wallow. Knowing Kaiden, I wouldn't have a chance to wallow in peace.

"What do you mean, you couldn't? That doesn't sound like you."

"Look, it's complicated, okay?"

"Is it? Kaiden pushed.

I flung open the door to my dorm building and stormed away from him. "It is."

"Oh, come on!" He caught my door before I could shut it in his face and slipped in after me.

I groaned and dragged my hands over my face. Why did I have to have feelings? All of them were jumbled up inside me and making me feel sicker and sicker by the second, to the point of feeling like I might hurl up the half of my breakfast I hadn't wasted.

"You can talk to me, Ava."

When I met his eyes, and saw how seriously he was looking at me, I wanted to believe him. After everything we'd been through, why couldn't I trust him? Aside from his obvious big mouth, that is. I'd already confided many things in him, and he'd seen me at my worst just a couple hours ago.

I exhaled and sat on the edge of my bed. "I just don't know what to do.That asshole cousin of his thinks I'm some degenerate."

"You're gonna let that stop you? Since when does Raven give up?"

"But I don't even know where they took him. He hasn't called or texted me." I pulled out my phone just to check again. Nothing.

"You can do better than that. He *has* to come back around sometime, right? We could stake out his room, or something." Kaiden touched my shoulder. "Come on, we can do this."

"It's not that simple, okay?" I glared up at him and shoved his hand away.

"Why not?"

"Because they've all got powers like Falcon," I blurted the words out before I could stop myself. Kaiden's jaw practically hit the floor.

"What?! Wait—Wait—What does this have to do with Falcon?" I could almost see the little lightbulbs lighting up in Kaiden's head.

The last thing I ever meant to do was let the cat out of the bag—or more accurately, the Falcon. I was already halfway there, and Kaiden wouldn't forget what I just said. He was probably two seconds from figuring it out now. So, I might as well dish and tell all. If Dyami had his way, it hardly mattered anyways. Chay wouldn't be coming back.

I inhaled deeply and mentally prepared myself for the imminent freak out Kaiden was about to have. "Chay is Falcon."

"Wait, what?!" And I thought Kaiden looked shocked before. He was so shook he stumbled backwards and fell back onto the floor, staring up at me, agape. "Holy shitballs, Raven. How. Did I. Miss. This?!"

I told Kaiden everything, from the very beginning. I told him how Chay was the reason Raven existed. I told him about the incident with Chay when I was leaving with my dad.

Everything.

CHAPTER THIRTEEN

CHAYTON

DY LET ME calm down, stroking my hair and sitting on the bed with me. He whispered reassurances to me over and over, and even though I wanted to believe them, my overwhelming anxiety and inner turmoil wouldn't go away.

"Chay, there's more you need to know," he said, touching my shoulders and urging me back from him.

I shook my head vigorously. "No." What more did he really need to say? I couldn't take anything else. My heart couldn't take anymore, and anything else he said would no doubt make it worse.

I didn't want to hear anymore. My gut churned at the thought of what else he could possibly have to say, of how much more he could shatter me and my whole world further. All I could do was shake my head mutely.

"I'm so sorry that it turned out this way. But now that you're part of this, it's best you hear everything." He held my shoulders tighter, and began to speak again. "Long ago, monstrous beings threatened the people of earth. Our people tried to fight them to protect our home, but they were numerous, and powerful. Then a celestial being named Azrael visited our people. Azrael agreed to lend a group of our strongest the celestial abilities—wings and elemental powers—to help destroy the demons."

"Elements?" I wondered aloud. Did he mean like Ava's fire?

"We all have them," Ona chimed in. "Just like the celestial one! Mine is ice. Tah's is lightning, and Dy is wind."

"That's right," Dy said. "Fallen also have elements. That Fallen One, Avari, has the fire element."

I gave them all curious looks. For now, this strange new information replaced the ball of anxiety in my stomach. "But why don't I have an element?"

Dy brushed his finger over my left ear, looking closely at my earring. "I think there must be something wrong with your gift. You should have an element like we do, and be able to see the demons."

So all this time, I was meant to have an elemental power, like Ava? If I was able to see demons, I could fight, and then I could protect Ava… Or, if what Dy said was true, protect myself *from* Ava. I shuddered at the thought. I didn't want to believe that. Was it really something imminent that Ava couldn't control?

Dy touched his necklace and his wings burst forth. They were shades of dark brown and black, with white tips. I couldn't help staring in wonder at them. "This power is meant to fight the demons, Chay."

"Fight the demons?" I echoed, insides churning again. The onslaught of unwanted memories was threatening to overtake me, along with all my doubts. I put my hands on my head.

"Yes. Azrael gave us this power to fight. Our ancestors passed down their gifts to us, so we would be able to fight again if the time came. We can all fight them, together."

Tah and Ona stood and came to Dy's side. Ona touched his bracelet, and Tah touched his ring, bringing their wings forth.

"Together?" I stared at all of them now. They all looked so much more confident, and stronger, than me. Stronger than Falcon. I'd been living a lie. Falcon had never been meant to be some shining hero of the people. I wasn't strong enough for that, or this, was I?

"Fight with us, Chay," Tah said.

"Yeah, let's do this!" Ona put his fist up.

"What do you say, Chay? Will Falcon join us?" asked Dy.

"I...I don't know." I clutched at my head again and squeezed my eyes shut.

I wished all this would just go away. I didn't want any of it. I wasn't even sure I wanted this power anymore. All it brought was pain.

Part of me wanted to say yes, despite being terrified. I didn't want to feel helpless anymore. Then, I thought about my reason for that: Ava. I wanted to be there for Ava, for him not to have to fight. That might not be possible anymore. What if I wasn't meant to fight for him, but against him? Just the way we'd started this.

Dy touched my shoulder, pulling me out of my whirlpool of despair. "I know it's a lot to think about. You worked so hard to come here, and I'm asking you to abandon that."

My heart clenched tight at the word abandon. "I'd have to leave?"

"We can't all stay here forever, Chay," Dy said.

"But aren't the demons all here?" I asked.

"For now. We'll take care of the infestation here before we move on," Dy said.

"There's only an infestation because of *him*," Tah growled.

"Him?" I asked, staring between Tah and Dy curiously. Tah's brows were pinched together, his teeth gritted. He looked like he wanted to punch something.

"Avari. Your..." Dy trailed off and grimaced, as if it was painful to admit what Ava was to me.

"My boyfriend." The monster, according to Dy. My chest ached. "Dy, you really think he's going to turn into a monster?"

Dy's glare withered, and he looked at me with sympathy now. "It's not just that. He's making it worse, Chay. Every time he uses his power, it's a beacon to the demons. The Fallen Ones and the demons call to each other. All he's doing is calling more to him. It's only a matter of time before he turns into one of them."

I shook my head fervently at the thought. "Ava wouldn't. Those things are monsters. Ava's not... He's not." I couldn't bear the thought, let alone say it.

"Chay..." He touched my shoulders again. I wanted to pull away, but couldn't find the strength to. "All the Fallen are demons now. They all either changed, or perished. It's why the celestial one had to step in and cull the demons."

That couldn't be right. Could it? Ava's father was one. He fought the demons. I couldn't believe that Ava would turn into something so heartless and evil.

"That's not true. Ava's different. He's good. I know he is. And his father, he's a Fallen One, too, who fights the demons."

Dy touched my chin and tilted it up so I would look at him. "Did Avari tell you all this? How do you know it's true?"

I'd only met his dad once, but he'd saved my life, and he'd understood what Ava and I meant to each other. If he had any ill intent, wouldn't he have kept Ava from staying with me? What was I missing?

"Ava wouldn't lie to me."

"He's never lied to you?" Dy looked skeptical.

I couldn't say no. We'd kept secrets from each other. We were done with that now, though. Weren't we? My pause was more than enough for Dy.

"He can't be trusted, Chay. For all you know, the seed of evil could already be growing within him and his father. It's better if you end things now, before you get hurt."

That wasn't fair. It wasn't like that. I wanted to tell him, but I couldn't find my words. I squeezed my eyes shut, begging this nightmare to end. I tried to pull out of Dy's grip, but he held onto my shoulders tighter, pinning me under his iron stare.

"It's only a matter of time. A matter of when, not if," Dy said.

"The demons can't be trusted, or reasoned with," Tah added.

"No," I sobbed out, wriggling myself away. "No. He wouldn't." He couldn't. He just couldn't.

"The demons won't relent. They will never stop coming for him, until he either joins them or they kill him. Chay...I know it's a hard decision, but once we neutralize the threat in the area, I think you should leave with us. It's best to get as much distance between you and him as possible."

I didn't want to believe what Dy was telling me. He didn't know Ava like I did. He hadn't spent the past months around him, getting to know him, to learn the obvious truth: that Ava was a person with feelings, that he was strong and stubborn, and deep down, good. Even if Ava thought otherwise, it was true. What Dy was saying... It just couldn't be.

Surely, Ava wouldn't just turn into one of those monsters if he had any choice in the matter. Dy spoke as if it were inevitable. That no matter what path I chose, I would lose Ava, sooner or later. Fresh tears stung at my eyes. I didn't want to accept that.

When had Dy ever steered me wrong, though? All these years, he'd looked out for me, helped me manage and push through and learn how to function. What Dy was saying, he truly believed. And that frightened me just as much as the idea that Ava would turn into a monster.

"I'm sorry, Chay. It'd be for the best." Dy wrapped his arms around me from behind and held me as I bit back more sobs. He urged me to one of the beds. "You should get some rest. I know this was a lot to take in."

"No," I protested, but Dy was already helping me under the sheets, tucking me in, and shushing me. I was reminded of home, of after Chala was gone and Dy took care of me.

My eyelids grew heavier, and I drifted off to sleep.

AVARI

"HOLY SHIT! YOU'VE been holding out on me big time!"

Kaiden said and whistled once I finished telling him my story (which he'd interrupted several times).

"For good reason. Chay's secret wasn't mine to tell."

"You couldn't've told me!" Kaiden pouted his lower lip.

"You haven't exactly done anything to earn Chay's trust. You sought my friendship by means of extortion, and you're dragging me into danger every other day. You're not really on his good side, Kaiden."

Kaiden's eyes dulled a bit at that last comment. "That's for sure. It all kinda makes sense, now. No wonder he's always so serious." He flumped onto the spare bed and threw his arm over his face. "How did I not see this?"

"You can't tell anyone, got it?"

Kaiden pushed himself up and drew an X over his heart. "Cross my heart. I'll do my damndest not to blab!" He jumped up and shoved his hand out to shake on it.

I squeezed his hand firmly and pulled him closer. "I mean it. You take this to your grave."

"You got it, boss!"

I narrowed my eyes at him. He seemed genuine, but Kaiden was a blabbermouth, so I would have to keep tabs on him until I was sure. It would have been one thing for him to blab my identity weeks ago, when no one would have believed Falcon and Raven were dating. If someone were to find out now, it would destroy Chay's credibility. It would all be over for us.

Maybe it already was over, in a way. Chay was gone, and I had no idea if he was coming back. My chest ached as if it had a gaping hole in it at the thought.

"So, what now, boss?"

"What do you mean?"

"You're telling me, after all you guys went through, you're throwing in the towel now?"

My brows raised. I thought Kaiden would be happy Chay was out of the way. Not that he had a chance, Chay or no Chay.

"I told you I don't know where they took him. What am I supposed to do? He hasn't sent so much as a text."

"Well... If what you say is true, and they're all like Falcon, they're probably superheroes, right? What's one thing that draws superheroes out?"

My veins went cold. "No. Kaiden, no. Absolutely not." I flopped back on my bed and covered my face with my hands. "Just give it a rest."

"Aw, but—"

"But nothing. Leave it."

"At least try to text him again, okay?" Kaiden helped himself to the other bed again, stretching out and flipping on my TV.

I rolled on my side, facing away from the TV, and pulled out my phone. Nothing from Chay, so I sent a quick text: *Chay, please text or call me before you make any drastic decisions. Please.*

Tossing my phone aside, I closed my eyes and wallowed, while Kaiden flipped through channels on the TV. This wasn't how I expected to spend spring break, but here we were.

CHAYTON

I WOKE FROM my uneasy sleep halfway through the night, startled by familiar nightmares. The events of that evening flooded back over me in waves, and my body buzzed and fluttered with anxiety.

Dy was fast asleep beside me, and Tah and Ona were breathing evenly in the other bed, Ona's arm flopped over Tah like he was their pillow. They all looked peaceful in sleep. I exhaled deeply and ran my hands through my hair, messing up my already tangled braid.

I slipped cautiously from the bed, glancing back at Dy to check that I hadn't disturbed him, and started tip-toeing towards the door. I had to get to Ava, and talk things over with him. Get to the bottom of this. Pulling my phone out of my pocket, I saw it was dead and held in a sigh. Too often lately, I forgot to charge it. Ava could've been blowing up my phone. I had to go talk to him. He was probably worried sick, and I didn't want him to do anything reckless on my account. Even if...Even if I was leaving.

My hand had just grabbed the door when a voice made me jump. "Chay, don't go," Dy said quietly.

"I have to talk to Ava about this." I turned the knob.

His footsteps signaled his approach. I didn't turn to meet his gaze. His hand closed over top of mine, a slight comfort that eased my churning nerves. "It'll only make things harder for you. Believe me. I wish things were different, for your sake. But it's better if you make a clean cut and leave now. The sooner the better, and easier it'll be." His voice was so assured, a steadying force in my unsteady mind, just as it always was all the times he had to talk me down when I was spiraling.

"It's already too hard. I can't just leave him like this. I need to talk to him."

"I can't let you go. It's too dangerous. He's too dangerous." For him to speak with such certainty, he had to believe that was true.

Was Dy right? Was Ava really so dangerous that a clean break was the only way? Dy *was* usually right. My c est ached at the thought of not having one last conversation with Ava, but Dy was only looking out for me. Always looking out for me. Always grounding me when I was falling.

Fresh tears pricked at my eyes. My mind was falling into an abyss again, swirling in chaos, with no end in sight. "Ava wouldn't hurt me," I protested, uselessly, as Dy squeezed my hand and removed it from the doorknob.

"He's never done anything to hurt you?"

I kept my head down, guilt-ridden, squeezing my burning eyes shut tight. Why was I a horrible liar? "It's not like that. He cares about me," I evaded.

"Come on," he said, leading me back to the bed, my wobbly legs betraying me and letting him. "Rest. We'll get to the bottom of things tomorrow."

"No," I muttered, only half-heartedly. My body felt like mush, and I couldn't fight back as he tucked me into the bed again. I was too lost in my anguish.

He held my hand, anchoring me there until I nodded back off.

AVARI

"YOU SURE YOU don't wanna hit the beach?" Kaiden asked the next morning, after I'd made no efforts to even leave my room. He'd stayed all night, and I'd pretty much ignored him the whole time. I hadn't told him to leave, though. I didn't have it in me.

"Positive." The idea of the beach especially sounded absolutely terrible. Sand was gritty and got all over everything, and water was cold. I far preferred wallowing to that. I checked my phone. Still nothing from Chay. I tried pressing call, only for it to immediately go to voicemail.

"Come on! It might take your mind off things."

"No. Go by yourself if you want to go so bad." I wanted nothing more than to lie here and fade away. There was no point. What would I do if he didn't come back? Ache stabbed at my chest and I squeezed my eyes shut. Well, I had made it seventeen years without him. I'd have to learn to live without him again.

"But that's no fun!" Kaiden whined.

Kaiden would still be here. I grimaced at the idea of no one but Kaiden for company. I had to take frequent breaks from him and his extraness.

"I need a wingman, you know? The beach is boring by yourself!" Kaiden sat up and winked down at me.

I rolled away from his grinning face. "You're hopeless. Just leave if that's all you're going to talk about."

"And let you mope all by yourself?" Kaiden poked my shoulder. I swatted at his hand.

"Yes, exactly. Buzz off."

A few moments passed, and Kaiden was eerily quiet. For a moment I thought I finally got through to him, or maybe upset him, or that my wish had come true and he'd left.

"Ava."

Something about his voice gave me goosebumps. I sat up. "What's wrong?" The wide-eyed, paler than a ghost look on his face told me something wasn't right.

Closing my eyes, I tried to reach out with my demon sensing feelers or whatever, more carefully this time, like a person feeling their way through pitch black. Then I felt it.

Pure and sinister, growing steadily more intense. I opened my eyes and withdrew my unseen feelers when a sharp pain shot through my temple. More demons were headed this way. Queasiness spread through my gut. It was so strong. How many were there? Or was it a greater demon? I gulped down the bile that threatened to rise in my throat.

"Do you feel it? They're headed this way!"

CHAPTER FOURTEEN

CHAYTON

"DANG, THIS PLACE has some pretty wild stuff on the news!" A cheery voice said, jarring me from sleep. For a moment, I thought I was in Ava's room, and Kaiden had turned on the morning news, waking us up. I half expected Ava to slink an arm around me and groan. Then the voice spoke again, killing that thought. "It's nothing like back home!" Ona said, and the illusion was fully shattered.

"Hmph," Dy grumbled.

Something about Ona and Dy reminded me of Ava and Kaiden. That begrudging, yet deep down flame of kinship, friendship. Like Ava with Kaiden, Ona earned friendship quickly with Dy, out of nowhere. It'd been hard won between Ava and me. Yet for Kaiden, it seemed so easy. A pang of longing formed in my chest for Ava, who was probably with Kaiden at this very moment. I winced at the thought. I should be with him right now, not Kaiden. And now, I might not ever have the chance again.

"It's unsurprising Chay got caught up in big city life," Tah added. "Off playing superhero, ignorant of the real threat." I grimaced, a stab of resentment running through me. Was that really what Tah thought of me?

"Shh," Dy shushed him, glancing in my direction.

I sat up then, glancing at Tah in the cushy chair in one corner, who immediately looked down at his phone, and then over to where Dy and Ona sat at the small table. Dy had the local newspaper in his hands, and Ona was munching on a granola bar.

"Hey, coz." Dy smiled at me.

"Hey, Chay! Good morning!" Ona said brightly, flashing a toothy grin. I noted Ona was wearing a *He Today* pin again as he shot his hand up to wave enthusiastically.

"Morning," I said, sounding more like Ava, with his usual dullness towards everyone but me. I groaned, rubbing the crusty bits of dried tears and sleep from my eyes. I really wanted a nice hot shower, even if it didn't wash all my worries and woes away.

My chest ached anew at the thought of Ava. It seemed like we were a part of each other's lives for longer than half a year; our threads were already so thoroughly tangled together. I doubted I could ever unravel them.

Was this how it had been for Ava when he was going to leave? I couldn't take this ache. All the super strength in the world wouldn't be enough to bear this burden. How could it? How did you carry on when you couldn't be with the person who made you happy, yet they were still out there, living their life without you? How could you live when you were aware they had to carry on, too, both of you only a shell of a person? Would the ache ever fade?

I headed to the bathroom to relieve myself. When I came out, Ona smiled at me again. Dy looked up at me from his newspaper.

"You okay, coz?" He asked, eyebrows pinched with concern.

"Want a granola bar, Chay?" Ona unwrapped a granola bar, holding it out. I took it from him, though I didn't feel like eating anything, my stomach in knots.

"You're really not going to let me go talk to him?" I asked Dy.

"Would you even be able to leave, if you did?"

I frowned. When we were kids, him a more reckless teenager, and me still a small child, I used to follow him around everywhere, asking him question after question. He was always proudly answering, as if he had all the knowledge in the universe. Back then, I believed every single word out of his mouth. Now, I wasn't sure what to believe. I wanted to at least give Ava a chance to explain things. Dy seemed certain that was a bad idea, though.

"Sorry, Chay," Dy said. "I don't trust him. He's too close to one of *them*."

"But he's not!" I gritted my teeth and squeezed my hands into fists, crumbling the granola bar. "I trust him. Please, let me just go talk to him."

"He can't be trusted," Dy reasserted, giving me a hard look.

"You feel that?" Ona said, clapping his hands together. "There's a bunch of 'em!"

"Are we going to fight?" asked Tah.

"Yes." Dy stood. Ona grinned and jumped up as well.

Tah sighed. "That Fallen One is who they really want. We should let him and the demons fight it out, then take care of the riff raff afterward."

Dy shook his head. "We can't risk them hurting innocent people. Tah, you stay here with Chay. Ona, with me."

"You're going to leave me here?"

"Sorry, Chay. Until we get you trained more properly, it's safer for you to stay put. I don't want you running into trouble."

Or Ava, I thought, begrudgingly. So instead, he was going to stick Tah with babysitting me?

"But Dy..."

He put a hand on my shoulder and squeezed. "I'm sorry. It's for the best. Trust me."

It seemed my hands were tied at the moment. Tah stood tall, and gave me a stern look. I wasn't going to get past him.

Once they left, I sighed and fell back down on the bed, surrendering to my sentence and my despair and whirling anxiety.

AVARI

KAIDEN SHOT TO his feet.

I wasn't even sure how he could stand right now. I flopped back down on the bed.

"What are you doing? We have to fight them!"

"Help yourself. Fighting those things has gotten me nowhere but in deeper shit."

Besides, it hardly mattered anymore. What did I care if the demons leveled the whole campus? It wasn't like Chay was here. I didn't have anyone to protect. All I wanted now was to mope away the rest of my spring break, and then mope some more, and some more, until it didn't hurt anymore. However long that would take. Maybe forever.

"They'll level this place! Don't you care about that?"

"Not really. I'm the bad guy, remember?"

"You're not. If you were really all that bad you'd have done far worse things in your stint as Raven."

He had a point. That didn't change things, though. That didn't change the fact that Chay was gone.

"Whatever. Since when do you care? You're no saint, either, knife boy."

"I'd rather fight and live to see another day myself than give up on everything. Plus, it's like we're vigilantes outlawed by the media, which is like, way cool! Don't you think?"

"Not really. It's annoying."

People in general were annoying. The news was worthless. They always got shit wrong. They made my dad out to be a bad guy, as well as me, even after I wasn't. People detested and feared that which they didn't understand.

"Oh, come on! Do you think Falcon would give up, even if the media were against him? Do you think Chay would give up?"

"Don't you *dare* bring Chay into this. It doesn't concern him."

Kaiden stepped closer, leaning over to look at me. "Doesn't it, though? If Chay were here, what do you think he'd do? Do you think he'd let the people here get hurt? Chay would want to help people. *Falcon* would."

I waved him off and turned on my side. "Well, Chay isn't here."

Kaiden grabbed my shoulder and flipped me over on my back again. "Well, I'm still here, and I'm telling you. You can't give up, Ava. Don't give up on life. Don't give up on the world. Even if they've given up on you. You can be good. You *are* good. You can still be the hero of this story."

My eyes went wide. For a long moment, I was only able to stare at him, stunned. This was the most heartfelt, righteous speech Kaiden had ever given. He sounded more like Chay than Kaiden right now, with all the talk about how I really was good deep down and all. And here I thought Kaiden was one of the bad guys of this story, as well as me. Somewhere along the lines, we'd turned into reluctant heroes. Anti-heroes. Vigilantes.

But maybe, I'd never really been the bad guy at all. Chay hadn't thought so. Apparently, Kaiden didn't, either. Ironic. Here I thought he admired me because of my villain status. Maybe Kaiden was right.

Chay or no Chay, I had to do the right thing. Who else could? Perhaps, all along, this had been my fate, like my father. This was inevitable. I couldn't run from it. The right thing, the *good* thing to do was to fight.

"What do you say? Are you coming?"

I took Kaiden's hand and let him pull me up. He beamed at me and gave me a peck on the cheek. My face burned and I immediately wiped it off. I'd let that one slide this time.

"Let's do this," I said.

We hurried to our spot beneath the trees. Kaiden was hopping on his feet with excitement, while I was an anxious ball of nerves. He wouldn't stand a chance against a greater demon. I had to keep it away from him. At least he could hold his own up against the lesser demons.

Kaiden donned a red mask lined with gold trim, beaming at me as he pulled up his hood. I pulled off my shirt and put on my sleek black domino mask.

"Want me to stow your shirt for you? I got plenty of

pocket room~" Slash waggled his eyebrows at me. I handed it to him and he stuffed it in his hoodie. "Ready for this?"

"As I'll ever be," I said, and took a deep breath to steel myself for the coming battle.

Slash clapped his hands together, grinned at me, and then outstretched his hands. "Carry me, hot stuff."

I scowled at him. "Never call me that again, so help me God, or I'll never take you flying again."

Slash only snickered at that. I sighed and picked him up, taking off into the air and towards the looming evil, with some guidance from Slash, since I was still new to this.

"They're almost here!"

I could feel them now. The sensation was so strong that I was surprised I could even flap my wings, or keep my grip on Slash. Pulses of sinister energy sizzled through my limbs, amping up my abuzz nerves even further.

I could do this, I reminded myself. I took out greater demons by myself before and I could do it again. Probably. Maybe.

I've got this. It'll be fine. I'll be fine.

The bright red mass of demons came into view. I kept flying towards them, until they became clearer. There were three lesser demons and one greater demon. *Deep, slow breaths. I can do this.*

"Hold on tight," I told Slash. As soon as his arms tightened around my neck I stuck my hand out and conjured a small flame. "Come and get us, you bastards!" I let the flame loose in their direction, then about faced and took off as fast as I could.

I led them away from the campus and towards the Bay. We had little choice whether or not to make a scene, but at least the campus would be safe. I would hate for the demons to ravage the Campanile or something else around the area that I loved, like Little Gem, or the burrito place. There would be no end to my wrath were I forced to live without Avari's special.

"They're gaining on us! We'd better land soon if you want my help!" Slash brought me back to the present.

"Right," I said and started to descend. Slash's help would be nice for the lesser demons. No way was I letting him anywhere near the greater demon though.

I landed on a flat roofed building, put Slash down, and prepared to face the demons. There was no more running or hiding. I couldn't escape this. I was both the villain and the hero, the darkness and the light, the sinner and the saint. I was the anti-hero. This was my fate.

"Let's kick these demons' asses!" Slash said as he whipped out a pair of knives like it was second nature. One of them, which he twirled around on his finger, was rainbow colored. He was *so* extra sometimes. All the time, really. Guacamole, as he'd put it.

"You take care of the little ones and I'll lure the big one away."

"Aw! But I wanna see you fight it!"

"No chance. It's too dangerous. You just be careful, okay?" That one was all mine. Unfortunately. That thing would tear Slash limb from limb if it got its hands on him, a fact Slash should've been well aware of after his concussion. He was no match for one of those.

"I'm always careful!" Slash beamed at me, and I rolled my eyes.

"Says the one who got the concussion." I spread my wings out. "I won't go far, but you'd better not let those demons get the best of you while I'm gone."

"Never! Remember who you're talking to? The knife extraordinaire, Slash!"

"Right. Slash 'em up, then, Slash." This was my calling, I supposed, so I might as well have fun with it. What did I have to lose?

"With pleasure!" Slash snickered, seeming to enjoy my pun.

I hovered in the air as the demons approached. A knife zinged past me and struck one of them in the eye, throwing it off balance. It fell down with a heavy thud. I pulled together a fireball for the big one and threw it at its stomach.

"Hey, over here, you big piece of shit!"

That got its attention. As soon as it started coming towards me, I flew away, leading the slow, gargantuan beast on an almost leisurely flight. Soon enough, the thing would rear its nasty side and speed up on me, same as before. Tricky suckers. Once I led the thing further away, I turned to face it. If I could manage to gear up enough fire power before it got too close, that might take it out in one fell swoop.

Nerves on fire, I brought my hands up and let my fire come, as much and as hot as it would. Heat and crackled black traveled through my arms. Though it was only a moment, in a flash the demon had closed the gap between us, too soon, and head butted me before I could bring my fiery wrath upon it. Downward I went through the clouds, struggling to stay in the air. Barely, I managed to catch myself before I could plow into a building.

Damn, my head was pounding. The demon pummeled into me again before I could recover, throwing me for another loop. It tackled me down onto the rooftop of a building, bearing its full crushing weight upon me, staring me down with its empty red eyes and its charred, ugly face. Was this it for me?

No. I couldn't let this thing win. I wouldn't.

"Get! The! Hell! Off! Me!" I said, thrusting balls of fire into its chest with every syllable I spoke. Every word took excruciating effort with the demon on me. I worried my lungs would collapse at any moment.

No matter how many times I pummeled the thing, it didn't budge. Maybe I was kidding myself, and taking these stronger demons on alone was too reckless. Had I been lucky before? Now, trapped beneath the behemoth, I didn't measure up.

The demon pounded me in the face, and I cried out. I thought Falcon punched hard. His fist was nothing compared to this. My ears were ringing, and my head was spinning. The edges of my vision started blurring. Where had I gone wrong? Letting this damn thing get its clutches on me, that's where.

Sorry, Slash. I hope you're faring better than me.

Only a miracle could save me now. Whether it be divine or demonic intervention, I didn't care at the moment. Anything would be welcomed, anything better than this. Not like this. Not before I could see Chay again. Would I ever see him again, though?

As I was contemplating that, the demon froze. Literally. Ice shards bloomed over the behemoth, encompassing it until it was encased completely, unable to move a muscle. The demon, now an ice sculpture, was helpless to do anything. Its red eyes were wide, petrified. God damn, it was heavier than before, too.

Then, a strong wind whisked over the demon ice sculpture to knock it over. The ice, and the demon encased within, shattered into a myriad of shards. They glinted and sparkled and shone like prisms as they scattered, the smaller specks blowing away, gone with the wind, while the large crystals fell around me.

Wing beats came from above me. Two figures alighted on either side of me, donning familiar feathered masks. The owlish one I recognized as Ona, while the other one was brown and white, framed by telltale dark hair greying at the temples—Dyami.

"*You*," Dyami hissed out in a low, disdainful voice.

"*You*," I echoed his contempt.

"Hey Avari!" Ona waved at me, huge doe eyes glinting and a friendly smile on his (their? they weren't wearing their pin currently) face, as if they were running into an old friend rather than a new enemy.

"What do you think you're doing?" Dyami asked, glaring down at me.

I sat up and shot him a derisive glare in return. "Fighting demons? You?" I spoke with a nonchalance in my voice, as if he was an old friend who'd just run into me and asked me 'What's up?'.

Dyami lunged at me, gripping my shoulders and slamming me down. "Do you even realize what you're doing?" He spat as he pinned my wrists to my sides. I growled at the unwanted contact. My fingers itched with the desire to fight back, to wrest myself from his hold.

I stared sourly up at him, unflinching at his harsh words despite my insistent, burning (almost, but not quite literal) need to get away, to escape his clutches. "Of course I do. You caught me at a low moment, but I've dealt with these things before. I know what I'm doing. So back off." I pushed against his grip. It only tightened. I gritted my teeth, seething. I could use firepower to escape. In my veins, the fire was already roiling, ready to boil over at any moment. How easily could I ruin him? I refrained. I couldn't do that to Chay, as much as Dyami stirred my rage. "And tell me where Chay is," I added.

"That's not what I meant! You need to stop fighting the demons," Dyami's voice boomed down at me, his teeth grit tightly.

"What am I supposed to do, lie down and die?" Screw that. Though the option of giving up on life was appealing over the last day, I certainly didn't intend to go out without a bang. Everything and everyone who'd taken my happiness from me would pay before I went down. Including Dyami, if he stood in my way.

"You're drawing them all to you. You're the reason that this place isn't safe for anyone. For Chay."

"Is that why you dragged him away against his will?" I sneered at him. "Why don't you let him decide what he wants, huh?" Did he think I was clueless about all this? Probably. In his eyes, I had no doubt I was little more than a nuisance, a no good, never do well, bad influence in Chay. Wasn't that judgement up to Chay to make? He was an adult, and Dyami was not his father. Blood ties or not, he could butt the hell out.

"And let him put himself in danger? Let him carry on with you, when you could turn into a soul-sucking monster at any moment?" His grip on my wrists turned deathly. I winced and clenched my hands into fists. My blood roiled, my fingertips itched almost painfully now.

"Don't you *dare* presume to know me!" I fought against his grasp harder now, letting my anger feed my fire rather than letting it come with a calm mind as my father had told me. Harsh winds wafted my heating fists, extinguishing my growing flames. "I don't know what your deal is, but you'd better let me go!" I snarled and arched and tried to throw myself uselessly at him. Rage burned within me, red and orange and hot.

"Dy," Ona whimpered out, "Maybe you should let him go, he's getting really angry."

"Owl," growled Dyami. "Ice, now, on his hands!"

"R-Right, Eagle." Ona—Owl, I guessed—put out their hands, palms facing me, and ice bloomed over my wrists and hands, halting my fire in its tracks.

"Let me go! Let Chay go!" I snarled out, jerking my head upward suddenly to butt Dyami's—Eagle's.

Eagle winced backwards. "Owl, more!" He barked.

Owl shot Eagle a withering look before biting their lip and sending more ice from their palms, down my arms and across my chest. I shivered.

"Just stay down. We'll take care of the demons. We'll take care of everything. Stay away from Chay."

"Like fucking hell I will!" The ice was so cold it burned. Cold brought back unwanted memories of a time when I was alone and helpless. Not so much different from now, really. So helpless. So cold. Unwanted, undesirable. A monster. Maybe that was all I was, in the end.

Dyami slapped me across the face, which only added to my overwhelming anger. I held in my wince as my eyes stung and my cheek burned. "You *will* stay away from Chay. Don't make Chay suffer because you're too stubborn to realize how much danger you put him in. We'll handle everything, and then we're leaving. *All* of us. Don't try to come after us, or find us, or else."

How much danger I put him in? That gave me pause. Could I deny that? My actions had almost *killed* Chay. Demons were knocking down my door every other day now, it seemed. I was a walking demon magnet, a disaster, and according to Eagle, one step away from a demon. I was the bad guy. I'd never been anything else, and it was naive of me to believe I could ever be good enough for Chay. That I could ever be *good.*

My wrists were so damn cold. So cold. My eyes squeezed shut.

I said nothing, made no protests as Eagle got to his feet. He thrust out his hands and wind buffeted me, tightening the icy grips pinning my body. Questions raced through my mind. Yet those questions were whispers compared to the screaming pain of my heart as Eagle and Owl flew away, thwarting my chances of ever seeing Chay again.

CHAYTON

WHEN DY AND Ona were gone, I went into the bathroom and holed myself up there without another word to Tah, his scathing words still stinging.

Sitting on the bathroom floor, I pulled out my phone and stared at the black screen. Oh, right. Dead. I exhaled and let the phone fall onto the bathmat. I doubted Tah would let me get away with charging it, even though he was always using his.

To avoid suspicion, I turned on the shower, hot enough to get the whole room steamy, closed my eyes, and thought about Ava.

The conversations with Dy were still running through my head, about things he'd never told me and things Ava hadn't told me. One thing stood out more brightly than everything else, though.

That was what Dy had said about my attraction to Ava. Could it be true, that the only reason I was attracted to Ava in the first place was because that odd, *different*, striking feeling I got around him meant he was a Fallen One, doomed to be a demon one day? This revelation put a whole new spin on things for me. My feelings warped into something different, tangled and distorted, all wrong. Had I completely misinterpreted things from the get go? Had I fallen for the bad guy, when I should have been running?

The hot shower was more appealing now. I pulled off my dingy feeling clothes and stepped under the searing spray of the water, sinking down after a moment and clinging to my knees. All the weight of everything kept bashing into me over and over, like a wrecking ball to a building. My heart couldn't take it, my nerves couldn't take it, and I couldn't take it.

When I finally was overheated and less overwhelmed, I stepped out of the shower. My clothes were still on the floor, dirty. I grabbed the robe hanging from the towel rack and slipped it on. Hopefully Dy or Tah would have something I could wear while mine were washed.

Tah was still messing with his phone. I went to one of the beds without a word and lay on it, still in the robe. Talking to Tah, even just to ask for some clothes, wasn't very appealing. He'd been so scathing, especially this morning with his comment about me getting caught up in big city life.

"Coz? You want something else to wear?" Tah was the one to speak first.

I shrugged, feigning indifference. Shuffling and zippers followed, and a moment later, some clothes dropped down on the bed beside me.

"Here, Chay."

I sat up and evaluated the clothing, just to avoid looking at Tah, staring at the grey t-shirt, boxers, and worn jeans before slipping the robe down to pull the shirt on.

"Hey, I'm sorry, about what I said."

"Don't worry about it. You're right. I did get caught up in things here." The reality of who I really was, who Ava was, and how all these pieces fit together, was much bigger than me. I'd been off in the big city playing hero and falling for my brooding lab partner, who I thought I was mysteriously drawn to because of love at first sight. Turned out, I was drawn to him because I was meant to fight against the peril his kind had created.

"I didn't have to be so harsh, though." He put a hand on my shoulder. "You didn't know."

He was right. I didn't know. I wished I still didn't know any different.

CHAPTER FIFTEEN

AVARI

HOW DARE DYAMI—Or *Eagle*, that's what Ona called him —tell me what to do. Eagle and Owl were long gone by the time I was able to heat up the ice enough to break through it, and with them, my only chance to find Chay.

Now, I hardly had any fight left in me. Eagle's words seared in my mind like hot brands on my skin, usually not so easily burned, but so easily made cold. My body shivered uncontrollably, and not just from the cold, as I removed the ice from my body. So, so cold. An involuntary whimper escaped me. Heating my hands, I melted the remains of the ice on my arms into water. Such a nuisance.

A nuisance. That was what Dyami thought of me. His words replayed once again in my head, smarting, burning, chilling. Don't try to find us, or else. They were all leaving, once the demons were thwarted. All of them.

Chay would be gone. And with him, a piece of my heart. The scorch marks he left on my heart would never fade, always sting, if I were forced to live out my days without him near. This was becoming more and more likely by the second, was all but imminent now. How could I fight back against three superpowered, basically, mes? Even more heart wrenching and gut churning, what if Chay *didn't* want me to fight back?

Turmoil froze me all over again, even though the ice was melted. Chills swept over me, even though there was hardly a breeze. I wasn't sure what was worse; never knowing the truth of how Chay felt in all this, or never seeing him again. Now I understood why he'd been unable to help going after me when I'd tried to leave him. Because now, faced with a world without him, I was thrown into misery.

I'm sorry, Chay. I wished I could tell him that.

Maybe I should have left then. If I was such a monster, such a nuisance, who could do nothing right and only put Chay in danger by being near him... Maybe this was our fate. What did it matter whether it was him or me who left? Perhaps this had only ever been imminent. We were light and dark, good and evil, saint and sinner. We were magnets facing opposite, forcing the other away at every turn, not meant to intersect. We were all wrong. Weren't we?

"Yo, Ava!" Slash's voice came from above, of all places.

Jolted from my spiraling state, I looked up towards his voice, towards the clouds. That shouldn't have been possible, for him to be in the sky... Out of the clouds popped a demon, out of nowhere, only upon its back, I saw a familiar, orange-hooded, knife-throwing boy.

"Look out below!" Slash bellowed out.

Here I thought I'd seen everything, that nothing Slash

could do would surprise me, and he came crashing down beside me riding on the back of a freaking demon like the chaotic being that he was.

The demon snarled in my face when it landed, spittling on me. Slash drew a knife and sliced its throat without hesitation, then hopped up and shoved the dying demon aside. The remains turned into ashes and blew away with the wind.

"What the hell?"

Slash grinned at me. "Pretty cool, huh? Sorry for the rough landing."

"You could have just waited for me," I sneered at him.

"Where's the fun in that? This was much cooler! Besides, I've got some inside info for you that'll help us get to Chayton!"

I eyed him intently. "You what?"

"On the way over, I bumped into his friends. You know, Mr. Tall Broody, and the excited one—"

"Yeah, yeah. I know who you're talking about," I urged him onward, in no mood for his wordy descriptions. "You ran into them?"

"Yeah. They fought off some more demons that showed up. Anyways, the excited one—Owl, I think?—accidentally blurted that they were headed back to the marina!"

"The marina..." Didn't ring any bells for me.

"Yeah!" Slash grinned. "There's only one marina nearby, and there's a hotel *right* on it! So that has to be where they're staying!"

"So what? It's not like we know what room they're in. We can't just march up to the door, and even if we could, they're not just going to let Chay go." That, and Dyami had made it perfectly clear that I would face dire consequences if I did come for Chay.

"I can make a distraction to draw them out, and then you can sneak past and go get Chayton!" Slash persisted with his ridiculous plans.

I shook my head. "Do you really think it'd be so easy? You make it sound like it'll be a cinch to just walk in there, and possibly walk right out with Chay. Dyami and his sidekicks would never let me do that. There's no point. Dyami pretty much told me to buzz off or he'd have my head on a platter."

Slash moved closer, getting in my face, in my personal space. "Come on! Don't you want the chance to at least talk to Chay? How do you know this is what he wants? Is it what you really want?"

Slash did have a point. His constant alacrity was confusing more than anything else. He'd been talking like Chay that morning, making me feel like a hero, and had just echoed my own thoughts. Of course it wasn't what I wanted.

I wanted to know what they'd told him, though. Had Dyami told Chay everything he thought about me? If I could just talk to Chay, even if only for a moment, maybe, just maybe, there was still hope for us to work things out. At the very least, Chay would be informed enough to make his own decision.

I hated that I was taking advice from Slash, of all people. Reckless, irresponsible Slash. If left to my own devices, I doubted I would have gotten in nearly as much trouble as I had the past couple months. Yet, he had a point. When had Slash gone and turned into some wise sage? He'd been making a lot of good points, lately. I needed to get to Chay and at least talk to him.

"Let's do this, then."

Slash bounced on his feet. "Yay!"

"Why're you so damn excited about this, anyways? Wouldn't you be happier if Chay wasn't around?" Things didn't quite add up. Slash was my fanboy. How had he turned into my personal cheerleader?

"What? No, of course not. Because you'd be unhappy."

I scoffed to hide my smile. When had Slash turned into such a good friend?

THIS WAS A horrible idea.

I felt it in my gut, yet my heart was at odds with my warring nerves. If I didn't get to the bottom of this, the regret and unanswered questions would steep within me forever.

Kaiden insisted on stopping back by his room to change into something "more promiscuous" as he put it. I wasn't sure why that was required, but I didn't object. If it helped with his master plan, then fine by me.

When Kaiden emerged from his room, he was wearing the tightest pair of pants I had ever seen him wear, black leather. My eyebrows raised. I was used to seeing him in baggy cargo pants and oversized hoodies. He also sported a matching leather jacket, and the shirt beneath was bright orange...and see through.

Kaiden beamed at me and did a twirl. "What do you think? Will I be a distraction?"

"Probably," I said, indifferent. I wasn't the utmost authority on what people would turn heads at. All my life I had challenged the status quo, gone against the grain. I didn't check people out, or think about whether someone was attractive. In fact, I hardly paid attention to most people at all. Kaiden's assessment of me being demisexual was likely true. It added up.

"Don't you worry. I'll keep those boys' eyes on me." He winked.

"I'm counting on it."

I hadn't ever been to the marina and hardly made note of it. Kaiden had to tell me where to go.

"I can't believe you don't know where the marina is!"

"Most of the time I'm flying too high to see that kind of stuff."

"Yeah, that's true! I wish I could fly! Riding that demon was pretty fun, but it didn't work too well."

I scoffed. "You're so reckless, you know that? You could've hurt yourself."

"But I didn't. So it's fine!"

"If you say so." His recklessness shouldn't have surprised me by then, yet Kaiden had been doing several things that caught me off guard lately.

We came up to the marina, and the nerves in my stomach grew almost unbearable. I landed behind one of the buildings and sat Kaiden down before retracting my wings.

"So, what're you gonna do to distract them?" I asked as I was slipping my shirt back on.

"I figure I'll make a big scene, yelling for them to come out, and you stay hidden, but watch for them to come out of their room and then—presto! We'll know what room they're in and you can sneak in!"

I was right; this really was a horrible idea. Not that I had a better one. I would just have to put my faith in Kaiden. That was a strange thought.

"Okay, let's do this then."

"Right! One fresh distraction, coming up!"

Kaiden pranced into the center of the surrounding hotel

rooms, humming as he moved. Keeping to the shadows, I watched and waited for Kaiden to hatch his fresh distraction, as he so eloquently put it.

"Hey, you guys that took Chayton! Come on out here, will you?! Come and show your faces!!"

I rubbed a palm over my eyes and sighed. Kaiden certainly *didn't* have a way with words. Whatever, it worked. He kept going on like that, while I scanned the doors, watching for any of them to open. A few blinds shuffled, likely innocent onlookers wondering what all the commotion was about. Doors cracked open, but no one emerged. Then, one fully opened, and Dyami walked out with a glare that could kill on his face, followed by the other two.

As soon as they were far enough from the door, I ran for it, not holding back any of my speed. Before the door could close, I managed to catch the handle and slipped in, closing it behind me and locking it. Kaiden was still out there yelling, until Dyami bellowed out for him to shut up. *Good luck getting him to be quiet.* I couldn't help smirking at that thought.

I took a deep breath and walked further into the room, heart leaping into my throat when I saw Chayton lying on the bed, back turned. It seemed as if it'd been an eternity since I'd so much as laid eyes on him. My whole body quaked with the enormity of everything, turning my stomach into a pile of mush. Chay. Beautiful, innocent, good, pure, and sweet Chay. What I wouldn't do for him, for all of this to just go away, or for us to be able to leave it all behind.

He hadn't seen me yet. I walked to the side of the bed. "Chay?"

He sucked in a breath and turned, sitting up to look at me. "Ava? What're you doing? You shouldn't be here."

"I came to get you out of here." I reached out for his shoulder and he flinched away from my touch. Sharp knives of anguish pierced through my heart.

"No. I can't." His gaze fell, and my heart with it.

"Don't be ridiculous. Of course you can."

"It'd be better if I didn't." Chay's words were almost muffled from the cacophony of my own heart beginning to crack.

This time I grabbed his shoulder and held on before he could move away, though he still winced. What had Dyami put in his head that had him cringing at my touch now?

"Can we at least talk about this? What the hell has that bastard told you about me?" I blurted out, my blood boiling. Whatever the hell Dyami had told Chay, he would pay dearly for.

Chay stared up at me, face turning sullen. "Ava, Dy is only trying to look out for me. He—He thinks it's best if I come home." His trembling lips turned down. His eyes were strained, brows knit together, and there were welling tears pricking at the corners.

"And you're gonna listen to him? After all we went through, now you're—you're just going to leave? You promised me he wouldn't change your mind. You promised." I swallowed the lump in my throat. My hands trembled, and I clenched them tightly. With anger, with fear, with turmoil. I couldn't accept this. I wouldn't.

He bit his lip and avoided looking at me. "I don't know. I didn't expect what he told me, Ava...The things he said were..."

"What did he tell you, exactly?"

"That you're dangerous, and you—you'll..." He choked on his words, a tear sliding down his cheek. The urge to reach out and wipe it away, and somehow with it, take all this pain away, was soul crushing. "You'll turn into a demon. He—He said all the fallen angels did."

So, that's what Dyami had told him. Something that I hadn't revealed myself. Not for any reason or out of necessity. I just hadn't thought to do so. I hadn't thought it would matter, and now, this dark secret of what the demons once were was coming to bite me in the ass. My not so glorious legacy. Dyami had some details wrong, though.

"Chay... I would have to try to turn into a demon." Even then, I wouldn't turn into one of those lesser demons, or any other type of demon.

He swallowed. His lower lip quaked. "So it's true, then. It's a possibility."

"Chay, no. It's—well it is true. The fallen angels, except my dad, turned into the original demons. But I won't. I promise."

Another tear slipped down his face, and this time, I didn't falter. I reached out and brushed it away. Chay shuddered and turned his head away from me.

"They keep coming for you—you can't stop them. What if you end up...joining them?" He clutched at his elbows, slouched down in a way that made him seem so insecure, so small. It ached to see him like this.

I took his chin and lifted it so he'd look at me, but he wouldn't meet my eyes. "I won't."

"What if it's not up to you? What if you're not able to resist forever?"

"That's ridiculous. I'll never be one of those soulless monsters, okay?"

"Is it really so ridiculous?" He worried his lip more, still wouldn't look at me. "Even so, you attract them. You're—"

Unable to take another moment of this absurd conversation, I crushed my lips to his in a bruising kiss. I wasn't sure what else to do. He wasn't *listening* to me. Chay just froze and let me kiss him. He didn't move at all except to tremble. I pulled away.

The cracks in my heart grew larger, ran deeper.

"You're just gonna let him get in your head?" My voice quivered.

"I'm sorry," he said, barely more than a whisper. "You haven't exactly been honest with me, Ava. Dy's just looking out for me. He only wants what's best for me, and for me to be safe."

I balled my fists so tight my nails dug into my skin and started stinging. My fingers burned as a raging, uncontrollable fire built within me. "What is he, your father? What about what you want? What you think is best for you? Or what I think? Why do you get to go play the hero and leave me here all alone?"

"Ava!" His voice boomed out—like Falcon, not like Chay—and his face hardened. Chay's hands clenched into fists, and for a brief moment I thought he might punch me like Falcon would, too. "Don't you *dare* talk like that. You don't understand how it was for us, growing up on the reservation. We *had* to look out for each other. I didn't have anyone else. Dy might as well be my father. He's the closest thing I've got to one. He's family."

Chay might as well have punched me, with the verbal blow he'd just dealt. All this time, I'd thought we were similar, and in truth, I was all wrong. He hadn't been alone like he told me. He'd been an orphan, but he hadn't been alone. Not like I had.

"You're right. I don't understand. Because *I* never had a family. I never had anyone."

Chay flinched, hard glare withering into a pained expression. "Ava—"

"Forget it. Have a nice life," I spat, turning on my heels. My anger bled through my words, my burning rage threatened to consume me in fire and it was all I could see, blocking out the aching and breaking of my heart, the screaming of my soul not to just walk away.

Because Chay wasn't listening. Chay wasn't like me. Chay didn't want me.

After everything we've been through. Of course Chay would choose his family over me. Blood was thicker than water, I supposed. And fire was but cinders in the wind.

"Have fun with your damn family. At least you have one," I said as I flung the door open.

This really had been a horrible, horrible idea. Despite my heart screaming, I walked away from the first person I ever gave a damn about.

"A-Ava..." He sobbed out.

I didn't look back.

My heart crumbled.

CHAYTON

MY HEART WAS shattering, yet my body was immobile. Ava left. *I* let him leave.

I was helpless to do anything except watch the person I loved walk out the door. Was this really it? This was the end?

I flumped back down on the bed and let my tears fall freely. Sobs cut through the air. How had things gotten so screwed up between us? Had this always been inevitable?

We'd wronged each other, over and over. There were

things he hadn't told me, and things I hadn't told him, too. I guess that made us even.

I hadn't told him I did have family. Not the closest of families, and quite broken, but I had one. I had Chala to look after me for a while, which I'd told him. Then I had Dy. Dy, who'd always looked out for me, who was always so encouraging and supporting, which I hadn't told him.

Fighting to stay together had only brought us misery, only stirred up all the broken pieces of myself that I'd worked so hard to keep together. How could we make things right? Could we even make things right? Maybe that was for the best, if what Dy said was true. Being here was dangerous. Ava was dangerous. Even if he didn't mean to be. He was a walking demon magnet.

We could fight the demons and keep them away from Ava, and Ava wouldn't have to fight. At least he'd be safe, even if we couldn't be together.

The door opened and I sat up, quickly rubbing the tears from my eyes, even though that was a futile effort—it was obvious I'd been crying. Dy came in, Tah and Ona on his heels. Dy's eyebrows were pinched together, his teeth clenched. "That guy is annoying. He was up to something, I know it." He looked around the room before his eyes settled on me. His expression changed from anger to concern. "What happened? Did *he* come in here?" Dy spat the word 'he' like it was venomous. He wouldn't even say Ava's name.

I couldn't hide the truth from my face. I nodded.

Dy came closer. "He came here for you. But you stayed?"

I swallowed and only nodded again. I wasn't sure I could speak quite yet.

"I know that must've been hard, but it's the right choice. It's for the best."

It didn't feel like it. It felt more like my heart had been

carved out, and I was but an empty shell of a person. My heart had gone out the door with Ava.

CHAPTER SIXTEEN

AVARI

I WAS FLYING over the park by the marina when Kaiden texted me.

Hey, where'd you go? Wait up!!

There were a bunch of crying faces following. I sighed and turned back, landing at the edge of the park.

Waiting at the park, I texted.

In a couple minutes, I spotted Kaiden running up to me. He stopped just short of slamming into me.

"What's going on? Where's Chay? What'd he say?" His face was close to mine, and I was in no mood for his barrage of questions. My heart was shattered, my chest ached, and I was maybe a few seconds from bursting into tears or flames, I wasn't sure which. My emotions were a tangle of anguish and rage. I could go off at any moment.

"He's...He's not coming," I managed.

"What? Why?"

"I don't want to talk about it. Let's just go."

"But—"

"I said I don't want to talk about it!" I growled and seized him by the collar of his jacket. My fist crusted over, and the beginnings of orange cracked across my veins. "Just shut up," I seethed out through gritted teeth. "I've had enough."

Kaiden, for the first time, looked at me with terror. I released my grip on his jacket, which was now singed, and he didn't say another word as I picked him up and took to the skies. The whole way back to campus, he was silent. I was beyond caring. In fact, I was glad I finally succeeded in spooking him, for once.

I landed us on the outskirts of campus by our usual trees, retreated my wings, and started walking away as I slipped my shirt back on.

"Ava—"

I whipped around and held out my palm. He froze, that surprised, terror filled look on his face again. It was just like that time I'd told Chay not to follow me. But he *had* followed me then, and he wasn't going to now. It was over.

"Leave me alone," I said, then turned around again and started walking back to my room.

Once I was finally alone, I closed my door behind me and leaned against it, sinking down to the floor and clutching my knees to my chest. I didn't try to stop the tears.

That had gone all wrong. I hadn't said anything I meant to say. Why did it all come out all wrong? All I did was make things worse.

Chay had once told me he wouldn't let me go. So why

had he let go now?

He broke his promise to me. He broke us.

And I couldn't fix it.

CHAYTON

DY PUT HIS hands on my cheeks, tilting my head both ways to take a closer look at my earrings.

"When you activate your power, do you only touch this earring?" He asked, finger brushing my left earlobe.

"Yeah."

"It's cracked. Maybe if we take it off, the right one would compensate."

"Would I be able to see demons then?" I asked.

"Yes, you should. Your elemental ability should manifest, and you might be stronger, too."

"I wonder what element Chay will be?" Ona interjected, a hand on their chin in thought that looked ill placed on their normally smiling, laid back face.

"There's only one way to find out," Tah said.

Dy looked back to me with an encouraging smile and gave my cheek a pat. "You ready for this?"

I nodded, then reached up to my left earring and removed it. Doing so after having worn it for so long felt strange to me.

"Now, activate your powers."

I touched my right earring and my wings appeared. Nothing felt different yet.

"What now? Should something else happen?"

"Try using your element."

"How do I do that?"

Ona stepped over and held out their hand. Ice whirled in their hand in an instant. "You've gotta let it come to you. Relax your mind and let the power come out."

"Okay..." I said, skeptical. Still, I had to try. I took a deep breath to steel myself, and closed my eyes as I held my open palm up as Ona had. I tried to clear my mind, and close off all the aching parts of my heart and soul. *Let it come to me.*

I opened my eyes after a moment when nothing felt different, looking down at my hand. Nothing had happened. I frowned down at it.

Dy gave my shoulder an encouraging pat. "It's okay. Keep trying."

"What else can I do?"

"Make sure your mind is clear, try to feel the air around you, connect with nature to beckon your element forward," Tah suggested.

I closed my eyes again. *Keep your mind clear.* Ava's face, stricken. Taken aback. Heartbroken. *Keep your mind clear.* Ava, walking out the door. Scathing words that ripped through my chest.

It was hopeless. I couldn't do this.

I opened my eyes. Nothing. I sighed. My heart just wasn't in it. *I let my heart go out the door.*

Dy urged me to sit down on the bed, perching beside me and rubbing my arm. The spikes of panic that threatened to overtake me eased, if only a little, under Dy's touch.

"Take it easy. It might not come to you naturally. Keep trying and don't stress if it doesn't happen right away. You'll get it eventually."

When Dy said that, I wanted to believe it. I wanted to believe that eventually, I would move on from this whole mess with Ava as well. Right now, though, it was all too much.

"Take a break. There's no rush to perfect it." Dy rubbed my arm again soothingly. The sting of panic in my chest eased back a little more.

"Okay."

After a short break, I tried to conjure my element again. I tried keeping my mind clear, as Dy said, and thinking of myself as one with nature, like Tah said.

"Hey, there's a park nearby! Want to try going there? Then you'll be like, closer to nature, like Tah says, you know, dude?" Ona suggested.

We all walked to the park. Tah sat on a bench, looking boredly at his phone, while Ona frolicked like a kid. I guessed they were still a kid, in some ways. Ona was a little younger than me. That, mixed with their bright demeanor, really gave them that child-like innocence. Their face even still had some of the pudge of youth, giving them a cherubic appearance.

Dy gave my back a reassuring pat and smiled at me. "Try to relax, and take all the time you need. There's no rush. Calm yourself, take in the nature around you, and keep an open mind."

"Right," I said, closing my eyes again.

Calm mind, open mind.

I tried to zone out Ona and their whimsy, pinching my brows together. Dy shushed them for me, and I relaxed again. Holding out my hand, palm up, I concentrated on the fresh breeze, the birds singing overhead, the sun warm on my face.

My hand started to tingle.

"Whoa! It's so bright!" Ona said.

I opened my eyes and immediately looked down at my

hand, only to be blinded by the goldenrod ball of light that had formed there. I hissed and threw my other hand over my face. My concentration was broken and the light faded away.

"You almost had it," Dy said.

"What was that?" I asked, lowering my hand. Bright dots flashed in my vision, like someone had taken a picture with a flash, or I'd stared up at the sun.

"It's the light element," Dy said.

"Light? Like the sun?"

"Yeah, basically," Dy replied, half-laughing.

"There's a lot we could do with that. It's a powerful one for sure," Tah said, finally intrigued enough to put away his phone and stand.

"That's so cool!" Ona said, leaning in close and looking at my face curiously. "Who would've thought the light element was hiding with you, right under our noses!"

He nodded. "I can't believe Chala had that one all along..."

Light.

I took that in for a moment.

It was hard to believe that I was even more like Ava than I thought before. The only difference was our powers were borrowed, and Ava was the real deal. A longing pain formed in my chest at the thought of him.

"What's the most powerful element?" I asked.

"It's hard to say," Dy said, "They all have pros and cons. Fire is the most destructive. Light is the most potent."

"I think fire is the coolest!" Ona chimed in. Tah jabbed them. "Ouch! What was that for?"

Tah shook his head and sighed at them. "You're not helping."

A spark of recognition flared on Ona's face. "Oh. Sorry."

My heart ached more. I tried to force the heartbreak away, stuff it down into the deep recesses of my heart, where maybe it wouldn't hurt as much.

"It's okay," I told Ona, even though it wasn't, and I had no idea how long it would take for it to actually be okay.

"You should be able to see the demons now, too," Tah pointed out.

"Yes, that's right," Dy said. "You can come with us next time we fight them. You don't have to fight, since you're still learning. Just stand back and observe. What do you think?"

"Okay."

Though I wasn't sure what to expect, I was curious about what the demons everyone else had been seeing all this time looked like. Would I see something of Ava in them? That thought was like a nail in my chest—harsh, stabbing, and paralyzing.

AVARI

KAIDEN BLEW UP my phone after I told him to buzz off. It was so annoying that I almost literally blew up my phone, until I remembered I could just turn it off.

I stayed huddled in my bed all night and all day. I wasn't sure what else to do, where to go from here. Could I just go back to the way things were before I met Chay?

I couldn't forget Chay. I couldn't ever go back to the (mostly) normal, social outcast with no cares life that I had before.

Never.

Knock knock knock knock knock. "Avaaaa!"

And not just because I also now had an annoying best friend.

I groaned and pulled my comforter up over my head. Why couldn't he learn to buzz off for more than like, a day?

"Ava! Come on, let me in!"

"Leave me alone, Kaiden."

I wanted to wallow. I wanted to fade away into nothingness. If I could forget every single moment with Chay, I would right now. I'd seal away my heart, and I'd keep that promise to the little boy who burned down the foster home: don't get attached to anything or anyone. Attachments only hurt in the end. I was fire, I was destruction, destined to burn everything I touched. Why had I ever believed I could have happiness? We were doomed from the start.

"Come on! Stop wallowing! Get up!"

Kaiden wasn't going to relent until he got his way. I wasn't sure what I even liked about him. Nothing right now, that was for sure. Right now, he was just being a nuisance interrupting my wallowing time.

I sighed and got to my feet, swaddling myself in my comforter and shuffling over to the door to let him in. I wasn't too concerned with how awful I looked. Kaiden had seen me at my most vulnerable moments already. Only he and Chay had seen those parts of me. Damn. I forced down the ache that jabbed at my heart.

Kaiden zoomed in and I went back to my bed, sitting down and huddling into my blanket more.

"You look awful!"

"Thanks, Captain Obvious. I feel fucking awful."

Kaiden plopped down right on my floor in front of me, jabbing a bag outward. "Well, never fear! Kaiden is here! With room service!"

"This isn't a fucking hotel, man, it's my room," I said, but I took the bag he kept wiggling in my face anyways, peeping inside to find a burrito, a hashbrown, some Oreos, and a small carton of chocolate milk. The whole nine yards.

Despite my state of melancholy and wanting to drown out the whole world, I pulled the hashbrown out—it was still hot—and took a bite. Crunchy potato goodness and spicy cheese filling burst in my mouth, and I took another bite practically before I swallowed the first. When was the last time I actually had eaten, anyways?

"Why do you insist on bothering me when I just want to be alone, huh?" I mused as I chomped into the hash brown, finishing it off in only a couple more bites, then starting on the burrito. It was a breakfast burrito, a concoction that was delightful and not my usual burrito choice, which I was now questioning why (perhaps because we always ended up getting waffles instead).

"Because I know you don't really wanna be alone." Kaiden skittered a little closer, looking up at me with that mischievous grin that was near constantly on his face.

"Yes, I do." I wanted to reach out and shove his head away, but that would require touching him, and I was in the middle of eating this glorious breakfast burrito, and still very ravenous.

"Surrrre you do." Kaiden jabbed my knee. I frowned deeply and jerked it away.

Something inside me snapped. Maybe it was my horrible day, my horrible past few days, really, but I felt the need to point out Kaiden's constant jabbing (literally). He'd joked about it before, never taking me seriously (as was normal for him) and maybe it was because we'd never had a serious conversation. Now seemed as good a time as any. It's not like things could get worse, and I was certain neither hell nor high water could drive Kaiden away from me, no matter what I said, at this point.

Unlike Chayton, who I'd royally fucked up with.

I shoved that thought away, focusing on the conversation at hand, the one that needed to be had.

I finished off my burrito and narrowed my eyes at him. "Look, Kaiden... You *are* my friend, but could you, I don't know, like...chill? With the poking and prodding and up in my face stuff?"

"Does it bother you?" asked Kaiden, grin fading, head tilting.

"Yeah," I snapped out immediately, then added, "I don't know if you noticed, but I don't really like being touched when it's not necessary. Do you think you could try to be a bit more respectful of that?"

Kaiden stared for a moment, perplexed looking. "But what about Chay? You let him touch you."

"Chay has *permission*." I rolled my eyes. "Chay is...was...different."

"How so?"

I wasn't sure how to explain the difference to Kaiden, between Chay, who I loved romantically, and him, who I cared about as a friend and nothing else. And I *did* care about Kaiden (even if I didn't always see eye to eye with him, or understand why I cared). Still, I didn't want Kaiden touching me when I didn't *feel* like being touched.

"I don't know, Kaiden. Chay's just..." Perfect. Imperfect. Everything. "You're both friends, you know, but he's my — was my boyfriend. " Amending that cut me to the quick.

"Oh, so it's because things aren't *that* way between us?" Kaiden wiggled his eyebrows for emphasis.

"What? No!" I growled, face feeling hot. "I just mean, he's different. And even with him, sometimes it's weird. Being close to people has always been a struggle for me. No one ever wanted me close until recently, you know? So it's overwhelming sometimes."

"Daw, look at you. You're so cute!" Kaiden was doing that starry fanboy eyes thing again at me.

"Oh, shut up," I barked. "Just, do you think you can start *trying* to be mindful, when it comes to touching?"

"All right, boss. For you, I'd do anything!" Kaiden beamed at me and gave a wink.

"I'm serious. Got it?"

"I hear ya. Now," Kaiden clapped his hands together, then leaned forward, planting his hands on his crossed legs where he still sat on the floor. "Why don't you tell your dear bestie all about what happened with Chay?"

I let out a heavy breath. He'd bug me until I did, so I might as well tell him. At least he seemed as if he was trying to keep what I'd just said in mind. So, with that out of the way, I started talking. "That it's better this way. And that Dyami wants him to come home."

"What? He's really going to just up and leave?"

"I guess so. He wouldn't listen to me. Dyami put all these ideas in his head about how fallen angels all turned into demons, and now he thinks I'll turn into one."

Kaiden stood on his knees, but remained a comfortable distance away, thankfully. "Whoa, whoa, whoa, wait...Is that true? Are you gonna just like, turn into a demon one day?"

"What? No." Had I never told Kaiden this, either? Might as well tell all now, I guessed. "Only the Fallen who hurt people for their souls turned into demons. My dad, and me, don't do that. We're not gonna turn into demons. So, put your knives away."

Kaiden heaved out a breath and flumped back down. "Oh, good. We mighta had a problem there."

I snorted. He wouldn't have stood a chance against me, but I wasn't about to tell him that. Not that it mattered. No demonic bone in my body.

"Anyways, I tried to talk to him, but he wouldn't listen to me. Dyami's got his talons in him so deep, I couldn't get through."

"And just like that, you're gonna give up?"

"What else am I supposed to do? If only I could get him away from Dyami, and explain properly to him..." I sighed and ran my hands through my hair. "But we're outmatched, here."

Chay and I were even, now. I'd tried to leave him because I thought it was better, because I thought he'd be safer that way. Now he was doing the same thing. I guessed I deserved that.

"And you're just gonna accept that?"

"What choice do I have?"

"You can rush in there, get back your man, and sit him down and explain! Do you really want this to be the end of things?"

"Well, no, but—"

Kaiden jumped to his feet suddenly. "No buts about it! Look, you've gotta at least explain the rest. You didn't get to. Once you have, then Chay can decide, once he has *all* the facts, and not just what the three birbskateers have put in his head."

I scoffed. "The three birbskateers?"

Kaiden shrugged and beamed sheepishly at me. "Cuz there's three of them, and they're all winged wonders, too."

"You're too much sometimes, you know that?" I shook my head at him.

"I'm guacamole!"

"Right, cuz it's extra," I said, unable to help smiling,

despite my overall despair. Kaiden was good at lightening the mood, I'd give him that much.

"You're stuck with me! Now, whataya say? Ready to go win Chay back over?"

What did I really have to lose, except Chay? Maybe it was hopeless, maybe I was hopeless. But damn it, if I didn't try, I would regret it forever. As much as I didn't want to admit it, Kaiden was right.

Kaiden really was a bad influence. Sometimes, though, I was thankful for it.

"Yeah, let's do this."

"Great! Let's go! I already have a plan!" Kaiden skipped out my door, and I had to catch up with him.

"So, what's your brilliant plan to get Chay back?" I asked, once we were outside.

Kaiden snickered and grinned at me. "*You* just take us on a little fly for now," he said, jabbing a finger out at me (but not touching) for emphasis.

"And then?" I gestured my hand, hoping he'd elaborate, which usually wasn't a problem for him.

"You'll see!" Kaiden grinned. I didn't like that grin. "Oh!" His face lit up, and he fished in his pocket, flinging something at me, which I barely managed to catch, and was hesitant to in fear that it might be a knife.

It wasn't. It was a set of keys, though there was a pocket knife keychain, of course. Kaiden grabbed out his phone, and a second later my phone buzzed in my pocket. When I took it out, I saw he'd sent me an address.

"Once you have Chay, just head to that address and use the door by the garage. And if you guys need any supplies for make up sex or whatnot I always keep that stuff fully stocked in my nightstand so have at!

"Ew, shut up, and let's go."

He skipped ahead without a care in the world. "All right! Commence operation get Ava's man!"

"Pff. You're confident," I grumbled.

"Aw, come on! Have a little faith! Let's do this!"

Right. Faith.

I rolled my eyes and followed him.

CHAPTER SEVENTEEN

CHAYTON

AFTER A FEW more attempts, I was able to form a small ball of light in my hand and hold it for a second before losing it again. It was only a little progress, definitely not enough to use in a fight.

"Don't worry, you'll get it soon enough. It'll take a lot of practice. All of us are different," Dy assured me. "Why don't you take a break and we'll get something to eat?" Dy clapped my shoulder, and started to walk with me, Tah and Ona following behind.

"Was it very hard for you? When did you get your powers?"

"I was about your age, and Tah was around the same time, so we practiced together."

"Then came Ona," Tah said with a chuckle.

"Then came Ona," I echoed. They'd come out of nowhere, showed up with Dy and Tah one day like he'd always been there, so natural and cheerful.

"We found them when we were out of town looking into some demon activity. They made an impression with their energy and curiosity."

Tah let out a half laugh. "That's one way to put it. Ona's an annoying little shit."

"Hey!" Ona protested.

When I glanced back, Tah had flung an arm around Ona and was giving them a noogie.

Dy had chosen Ona. Instead of me. To protect me, because I would've had trouble dealing with all this when I was barely getting by day to day. Ona blended with Dy and Tah seamlessly in a way I never had, even though they were closer to my age than Dy and Tah's ages.

Bright, energetic, and always smiling, they were all the things that I tried so hard to be, as Chayton and Falcon. But that wasn't actually me.

How could I ever measure up?

Dy ordered a pizza for us and we ate in the hotel room. The mood was surprisingly light now, all jokes and laughter. I remembered my many days spent with Dy and Tah where we didn't have much, but we had each other. It was a comfort that I could latch onto.

The mood changed within a split second. Dy's mouth pressed into a grim line. Ona stopped laughing.

"It feels like they're headed in this direction," Tah said.

"They're coming right for us! But how? Demons can't sense us," Ona said.

"Hawk, Owl, mask up," Dy ordered, pulling his own mask from his pocket.

"You can sense them?" I asked.

"Yes." Dy picked up his mask, too, and put it in his pocket. "We'll teach you that, too. Later. Right now, we've got some demons to take out."

"Yeah, let's get 'em!" Ona clapped their hands together.

They all started walking to the door. Dy looked back at me. "Come on, Falcon. You, too."

I swallowed. "But..." I wasn't sure what to do with all this information. Was I supposed to fight when I still was still learning?

Dy returned to my side to clasp my shoulder. "It's all right. You don't have to do anything but watch us fight, and learn. We won't let anything happen to you."

"Okay."

Dy reached in his pocket and pulled out something, holding it out to me. A domino mask, blue like my Falcon outfit. "Here, take this."

I put the mask in my pocket and let them lead the way. We walked until the coast was clear, then Dy gave a signal, and they all three touched their talismans, bringing out their wings. I followed suit. Once we were in the air, we put on our masks. It felt odd, not changing my whole outfit.

"The masks are a precaution, just in case. We try to keep our fights in the sky, though, so people don't see us," Tah said, flying up beside me. "Use our code names while we're wearing them, too."

If we were all seen, I couldn't imagine what the news would make of that. First, there was Falcon, and now there were five winged people, who appeared to be fighting some invisible enemy.

We were vigilantes, protecting the people from an unseen threat. One that an average person would never see coming. They weren't even aware of the danger.

Unless the threat hadn't turned into a demon yet... Or perhaps, Ava and his father might control the demons. *Ava, how could you not tell me about this?*

Pain blossomed like Ava's fire across my chest, and I squeezed my eyes shut to fight it off. I couldn't think about that anymore. I couldn't think about Ava anymore. It was over.

"We're almost there!" Owl shouted.

A figure appeared in the distance, and my throat tightened. Was it a demon?

Wait, no... It was a person. A person with black wings. It was Ava!

There was someone in his arms, and I had no doubt it was Kaiden. What were they doing here, though?

Patches of red trailed behind them in the sky. Birds, or bats? No...

Ava began descending downward, beneath the clouds, and the red figures followed suit.

"I knew it! He *is* with the demons! We've got to stop them!" Eagle waved us onward.

Hawk and Owl followed immediately. I hesitated, swallowing down a threatening wave of bile in my throat. My stomach turned in on itself. This couldn't be happening.

"Come on, Falcon!" Owl came back my way, waved for me. Reluctantly, I followed, their beckoning giving me enough of a jolt to kickstart me into gear. I was far from calm, though.

Raven had landed on the flat rooftop of a high building and put Slash down. Both were wearing their masks. He held out his palms and made flames in each one, brandishing that familiar Raven grin, and it was as if no time had passed since then, as if Raven was a mask that Ava could adorn at any time without a moment's hesitation.

Around them over the rooftop, the red masses—the demons—swarmed.

They were—They looked like actual devils, straight out of hell. I guessed that's what they were, though. Devils. Demons. Demons.

The demons were red, crackled like molten lava, like they might burst into flames at any moment. Their wings were leathery, taut, like bat wings, and their faces construed with nasty, gnarling snarls. They all had horns, some kinked and some curled backwards. One with horns that stuck straight up caught my eye in particular, made me flinch, made me remember.

My stomach churned and my chest burned, as if it had happened all over again. I had to touch a hand to my chest to check it wasn't damp with blood, and that I was still whole.

And all this time, this is what Ava had been fighting, and Kaiden, with no concern whatsoever. Ava hadn't ever seemed afraid, as terrifying as the demons looked.

Before me now, Eagle, Hawk, and Owl, were fearless, rushing in to meet Raven and Slash beneath the onslaught of demons who rounded like vultures to the kill.

I couldn't do this. I couldn't.

I froze up, hovering in the air, eyes fixed on the demons. All their eyes were focused below. Red eyes, like blood.

I trembled and clenched my shaking hands into fists so tight my nails dug into my palms.

I stayed still in the air, and watched.

Raven titled his head up at Eagle as he landed before him, a wide, wicked smile on his face. He held his arms out palms upward, in what I'd almost believe was a gesture of surrender, except he had fire in his hands. Slash stood beside him, all grins and two knives swirling in his hands.

"Do you have a death wish?" Eagle boomed at them.

"Perhaps," Raven said, flashing a gleam of teeth.

"If you had any sense you would've listened to me, and stayed away!"

"Ha!" Raven touched a flaming palm to his stomach. "Well, I don't."

"Then you leave me no choice!" Eagle growled and shot forward, right for Raven, tackling him down.

"No!" I hollered, rushing towards them. I landed beside Eagle and touched his elbow as his hands closed around Raven's neck. "Stop, Eagle! Stop!"

"We can't let him go, Falcon. I'm sorry, but he's too dangerous." He squeezed.

Raven's nefarious smirk faded as he began to wheeze. He swiped at Eagle helplessly. Wind surged around us, blowing out Raven's flames before they could ignite.

"No!" I grabbed Dy's arm. It was hard as rock, unbreakable, unmovable compared to my own. "Please!"

"I warned him not to interfere, and he wouldn't listen," Eagle growled.

"No!" I repeated again, unable to gather my thoughts and tongue into anything else.

I just couldn't let him do this, though. No matter what the truth was, I cared for Ava, and, naive as it was, I thought that if I left, at least he'd go on, even if it wasn't with me.

That might have been an impossible dream.

No, No!

I pulled at Eagle's arm with everything I had, because it had to be enough, it *had* to. He reared back his elbow, colliding with my head.

Everything spun as I went falling backward. My vision went blurry, and then black.

AVARI

I LANDED US on the Oakland Bridge.

"So... What's the plan?"

"Fire!" Kaiden exclaimed, throwing his hands upward.

"Oh my God, tell me you aren't serious right now." I groaned and put my face in my hands.

"What?" Kaiden looked at me as if I had five heads.

"You want me to attract demons? Are you serious? I'm supposed to be lying low, Kaiden. What will my dad think?"

Would he be upset with me? Picturing him angry drew a blank for me. I hadn't seen him angry. He was always calm and collected, a pillar of strength. Did he even get angry?

"How else do you expect to drag out the three birbskateers, dude? We can't just waltz to the hotel again. They won't be expecting this. We'll have the element of surprise, and then, *boom*—literally—and you run off with Chay! And I'll make sure they stay distracted so you two can hash things out. It's perfect!"

I sighed dejectedly and ran my hands down my face. "You will be the death of me."

"Do you have a better idea?"

I didn't. I sighed louder, lacing my fingers together and stretching my arms out until my fingers popped.

"Fine, fine. We do this, and then that's it. It's over. No more demon fighting, no more seeking out demons, nothing. Got it?"

"As you wish, boss!" Kaiden grinned and pulled on his mask.

I did the same, then put my palms out. "Stand back as far as you can." I brought as much fire as I could forward, going bigger than I ever had before. I flung them upward, rather than downward, so I wouldn't harm the structures or people.

It only took a couple rounds of that before some specks of red appeared on the horizon, growing closer and closer. We stood our ground a few moments more, letting them close the distance between us before I grabbed Slash and took off in the general direction of the marina. If Eagle and his posse could sense them like Slash could, which I suspected was the case from them showing up where the demons had been before, they'd feel us all coming.

"There's a lot of them, boss!"

"How many is a lot?"

Slash counted at a whisper, muttering quickly. "Baker's dozen?"

"Shit."

That was a few too many, but it couldn't be helped now. At any rate, it appeared our plan had worked. Four familiar winged figures loomed in the distance, speeding our way.

We landed and prepared ourselves, me with my fire, Slash with his gleaming knives and teeth. The demons swarmed above us, all around, watching, waiting. Eagle and his two sidekicks landed on the roof with us. Chay was still in the air looking down on us. Gone was his Falcon superhero getup; in its place wore his regular clothes and a blue domino mask. My heart clenched painfully with longing at the sight of him.

I will get the chance to talk to you, Chay. So I can tell you everything.

"Do you have a death wish?" Eagle hollered at us, voice deep, commanding, and booming.

"Perhaps," I said, flashing him a grin. If he was going to make me the bad guy, I might as well play it up.

"If you had any sense you would've listened to me, and stayed away!"

"Ha!" I planted a fiery hand on my stomach as I laughed. "Well, I don't." When it came to Chay, I was an impossibly reckless mess. There was nothing to be done for it.

"Then you leave me no choice!" Eagle growled and launched himself towards me, faster than I expected, and tackled me down.

"No!" Falcon's voice hollered out from above. Eagle's hands closed around my neck and began squeezing. Did he really mean to end me? I hadn't thought he'd react so violently, but apparently I'd underestimated his hatred of me, of the demons. "Stop, Eagle! Stop!" Falcon's voice said, closer now, right behind Eagle. My eyes were tearing up now so I could barely see him.

"We can't let him go, Falcon. I'm sorry, but he's too dangerous." He squeezed tighter, cutting off my wind pipes.

I swiped aimlessly now, fire extinguished by Eagle's wind over and over before I could gain any ground. I was left helpless to do anything but flail beneath him as he squeezed the life out of me. Shit, he was strong. Things started going fuzzy.

"No! Please!" Falcon's voice was so small, so helpless, so far away.

No. Please don't leave me.

Or was I the one being forced to leave him now?

"I warned him not to interfere, and he wouldn't listen," Eagle growled.

"No!" Falcon cried out.

Eagle loosened his grip, removed one hand from me, and then both as he spun around, away from me. I coughed and wheezed for a moment, blinked back dots of black, then sat up.

Falcon was on the ground, out cold. Had Eagle done that? He'd pulled back so suddenly. It could have been an accident. Still. He'd hit Falcon—Chay—and now he was on the ground, unmoving.

My blood roiled.

Eagle crouched down, touching Falcon's brow with such gentleness now that it only made my blood boil even more. How *dare* he touch my boyfriend with such tenderness, after only a moment ago knocking the shit out of him.

Around us, chaos had ensued as the others fought the hoard of demons I had gathered up; Slash with his knives, and Eagle's sidekicks with ice and bolts of lightning.

"What're you waiting for? Grab him and go!" Slash flung a knife past Eagle, who reared back to narrowly avoid it. A couple of demons landed nearby us, blood moon eyes on Eagle.

I hoped Slash knew what he was doing. Oh, hell. Who was I kidding? He had no idea what he was doing. He was always winging it, for not having wings himself. I just hoped he'd be okay. I had to leave things in his hands, and trust him to be the reckless, annoying distraction he always was.

I rushed for Falcon while Eagle was distracted by the demons, throwing him over my shoulder. Beating my wings as hard as I could, I tore through the sky and didn't dare to look back. Falcon was still out cold, and I hoped to God that he would be okay. Hopefully, he was just thrown for a loop. What happened with Eagle was just an unfortunate accident...right? I had no doubts in my mind that Eagle would harm me, but Falcon, his own flesh and blood?

I wasn't so sure.

CHAPTER EIGHTEEN

AVARI

I FOLLOWED MY phone's directions to Kaiden's house in a random suburb north of San Francisco.

His house was one of the many copies in the neighborhood, a garage in the bottom with the main floor above it. I fumbled with the key to the basement entrance, struggling to get it open without dropping Falcon.

Once I managed to get us inside, I made a B-line across the concrete floor for the bed and laid him down. I sat gingerly beside him and pulled off that ridiculous blue mask, tossing it aside, followed by my own. I'd had more than my fill of superhero garbage for today.

"Chay..." I stroked his cheeks, then gingerly felt his head for bumps or signs of bleeding.

This time, I'd be able to say the things I really wanted to say. I had to tell him the truth, so he could make his decision based on facts, not just Dyami's inaccuracies. Of course, I wanted him to choose me, I wanted him to stay. There was a possibility he'd still go, though, and that thought made my throat constrict and my eyes burn.

Chay's eyes fluttered open after a few moments. "Ava..." he said as his eyes focused on me.

I leaned towards him, hands still on his cheeks. "Chay, are you okay?"

"Mhm, my head's just a little fuzzy." He sat up and rubbed his head. "Wait, what happened? Where are we?"

"At Kaiden's house. Dyami knocked you out, and I brought you here, so we could talk."

"Why did you do that? I have to go back!"

"No. Just calm down and relax. You took a good hit to the head. Are you sure you're okay?" I gently urged him to lie back down.

"I'm fine. But Dy, he'll—"

"Shh. Right now, all I care about is you, and me. And we need to talk, too. Give me a chance to explain everything. Please?"

Chay bit his lip, but nodded. "All right."

"I'm not going to just turn into a demon. I know Dyami seems to think that, but I won't."

"Dy said it was inevitable. He said they'd just pursue you until you gave in."

"I promise you that'll never happen. He doesn't know everything about the demons."

His eyes were welling up with tears. "H-How do I know you're telling the truth?"

"Because I would have to devour human souls to turn into one, and I'll never do that. Did he tell you *that*?"

Chay shook his head, his tears dripping down the sides of his face. "Why didn't you tell me about this?"

I wiped a tear away from his face. "I'm sorry. I didn't think there was a reason to, because I was doing what you asked of me—I wasn't planning on fighting or anything as Raven anymore. I didn't expect any of this to happen, for things to get so out of hand. I'm sorry. You deserve to know everything, so you can make an informed decision."

"Ava..." Chay worried his lip, stared up at me with his glistening eyes.

"The demons that we've been fighting are called lesser demons, and bigger ones are greater demons. They're basically mindless monsters created by the Fallen that were once fallen angels, like my dad, but turned against humanity by devouring souls, and turned into demons. My dad is the only pure Fallen left, he thinks. He wanders the earth trying to cull the demons. So, that's it." I scooted back from him, towards the middle of the bed, a black and pasty blob upon the black sheets. "Now you know. I'm not with the demons, and they aren't going to tempt me to the dark side or anything. They're just monsters created by the original demons."

Chay sat up and stared at me. "You won't turn into a monster." He put a hand out, shaky, and splayed it gingerly upon my chest.

"I won't turn into a monster." I placed my hand over his.

Chay let out a heavy breath, followed by a half sob. I laced our fingers, squeezing his hand tight before bringing it to my cheek.

"I'm sorry about the nasty things I said. I was upset, and it was uncalled for," I said.

Chay sniffed and stroked my cheek. "It's okay. I'm sorry, too. Dy seemed so sure of what he was saying, and he's always been there to guide me, so I thought...I thought it was true. Even though I know that's not you. You're not a monster."

I held his hand tighter, took a steadying breath, because I had to say the next words. I had to give Chay a choice this time, now that he was fully informed. "If you still want to leave, I'll understand. I'm no monster, but I'm not perfect, either."

"Neither am I." He leaned our heads together and closed his eyes. "I'm not the perfect guy you thought I was. I'm broken, and I always will be."

"Look at me," I said, grabbing his face and pulling it back. "Nobody's perfect, Chay."

"I know that. But, I—I'm not who you thought I was. I'm not some smiling, shining pillar. I tried so hard to be that guy, but I'm not. And that's not who you fell in love with."

I pushed him down on the bed, pinning his arms on either side of his head. "I don't care about that, Chay. I mean, I love your smile. But you don't have to be happy all the time just for my or anyone else's sake. God knows I'm not. I'll still love you, no matter what. I love you because you're kind and caring, compassionate. Because you bothered to look at the real me, and loved me as I am. So I'll love you as you are, too."

"Ava..." His eyes glistened again, and he inclined his head towards me. When I let his arms go, he wound them around my neck and pulled me in for a kiss. His lips parted immediately, hungry and eager, and I clung to his shoulders as I let my tongue delve into his mouth to meet his own. My head swam as our tongues danced, fiery and ardent and needy.

CHAYTON

MY HEAD WAS spinning and my stomach twisted in knots —from Ava's kiss, from his touch, from his words.

He wasn't going to turn into one of those monsters, into a demon. He wasn't going to turn into a monster. He wasn't.

The relief that flooded through me at that knowledge overfilled my lungs, made my throat tight, and my eyes burn.

That meant that Dy had been wrong. How could I possibly go through with this and leave Ava after learning Dy's logic was inherently wrong?

I couldn't. I wouldn't. I didn't want to leave him.

Ava broke the kiss to speak. "Don't leave me," he murmured against my lips, as if reading my thoughts.

"I won't," I breathed out. I had no idea what would happen after this, if not leaving was even an option, but I wanted it to be true.

I latched onto the flicker of hope, that knowledge that, maybe there was another way. We could talk about this, we could sort things out. Ava could keep me and I could keep Ava. Maybe, just maybe. We could figure this out.

Ava snaked his hands up my shirt and I released my grip on him, raising my arms to let him remove it. Ava kissed me again immediately, pressing our bare chests flush with one another. It seemed as if it'd been an eternity, another life, since we'd kissed, since we'd been chest to chest, skin to skin.

If I could stay in this moment forever, I would. If we could just be here, like this, forever, no worries or anxiety or demons or anything else to wedge in between us, it would be so much easier. When I was with Ava, things didn't feel so awful. *I* didn't feel so awful. Ava was a beacon, a flame in the dark, leading me forward.

I want to be boring college boyfriends with you. There's nothing I want more.

Ava's hips pressed against mine, and I could feel he was hard. I remembered Valentine's Day, how we pressed against each other, and how I thought we'd do something else, but we'd been interrupted. I hadn't had the courage or the calm to attempt anything again, and I don't think Ava had, either.

I dragged a hand down his chest and stomach until I reached his waist and caught a finger on a belt loop.

"Ava?"

"Hm?" He pulled back, just a fraction, so our noses touched.

"Can I touch you?"

Ava was silent, still, and took a couple breaths before he nodded. "Anywhere you want. Just..." He trailed off, biting his lip.

I touched his cheek with my other hand. "Tell me if you want me to stop, or slow down, or anything."

Ava smiled and gave another nod, turning his head to kiss my palm. Our eyes stayed locked as I undid the button of his pants, then the zipper, and shimmed his pants down, just past his hips. Carefully, I rubbed my hand across the front of his boxer-briefs, looking at his face as he caught his lower lip between his teeth, and his eyes glazed over with arousal. He moaned quietly.

He was so beautiful.

I'd always thought so. He was striking, stunning, all harsh lines at a glance, yet when you looked closer, there was something smooth and serene underneath.

"Can we turn on our sides?" I asked him.

Ava nodded, and we turned together on the bed. When I touched him again through the fabric of his underwear, wrapping my fingers around him, he gasped and let his head fall forward to hide in the crook of my neck.

"Still okay?"

After an answering whimper and slight nod, I continued, one slow movement up his length, then back down. He drew in a quick breath, and I repeated the motion.

"Chay..."

"Can I keep going?"

"Yeah," he murmured into my neck, pressing a light kiss there with trembling lips.

I dipped my hand beneath his boxer briefs. Another gasp, and his whole body tensed, quaking, breathing slowly, shakily. So beautiful and vulnerable, and here, with me. I didn't deserve him. But he wanted me anyways. Not because I was a blood relation, an obligation. He wanted me for *me*.

"Touch me too," I said, almost automatically, and it came out as a whimpering plea.

"Mhm," he moaned his reply, nodding as he slid one hand down my chest, leaving a buzzing trail of electricity beneath my skin.

After a moment of fumbling with trembling hands, he managed to undo my pants, and then he was touching me, mirroring me with his hand beneath my boxers and wrapped around me. The world felt upended with one simple motion. Nothing else mattered but Ava and me. Together. Together.

And I never wanted to be apart. I never wanted to love anyone else. I'd never love anyone the way I did him.

AVARI

THE WORLD COULD come crashing down, demons could rend everything around us asunder, I wouldn't care, because Chay was right there with me, and that was all that mattered.

He pushed, I pulled. He bent, I broke. We were forever tethered, our fates connected in ways I never could have imagined.

We touched, we kissed, we grasped, and further and further I fell, lost in him. To be honest, I wasn't sure if I was doing any of this right. I had no experience to draw on, not even anything done with myself alone (I'd never had any desire to). Everything Chay did felt unmeasurably amazing, though. And when I mimicked the motions, a stroke of my hand, a brush of my thumb over the top of him, the tiny gasps and whimpers he made sent me spiraling, burning me to my core.

I was caught between feelings of pleasure and uncertainty. Did it feel wrong or right? Bad or just so good it was overwhelming? Doubt won, and I whimpered against Chay's neck, a mumbled, "Chay?"

He paused, and I lifted my head to look at him, despite the heat flooding my cheeks. His face was flushed too, his eyelids heavy.

"You okay?" He asked.

"Yeah, I think so. It's just…. Different. Good, I think. But I've never done anything like this before."

Chay pressed a kiss to each of my cheeks, and looked at me sweetly, needily. "It's all right. Take a second. Take as long as you need. I'm here."

I grabbed his hand and put it to my heart, wondering if he could feel the way it pounded. This was what he did to me. He broke me down, melted me, shined a light right through the dark recesses of my heart to my own light that, against all odds, lurked there. And he pulled that light forward. He made me want to be better.

Chay was my light, the only one for me. No one else could have braved the fire and flames.

"God, the things you do to me should be criminal."

Chay chuckled heartily and kissed me before taking my hand and putting it to his heart. It pounded heavily just like mine.

"You, too."

"You're an angel. You can do no wrong."

Chay smiles wide. "Thought I was a criminal? Now I'm an angel?"

"Mm, no…" I kissed his jawline, dragged my hand down his chest. "I said the things you *do* should be criminal." My hand found the space between his legs, and I traced my fingers over all the sensitive parts before wrapping my hand around him again. All the while I stared at him, the way his head fell back as I explored, giving me better access to his neck, which I took. The angelic moan that came from his lips was heavenly.

"Should say…the same….of you," he gasped out.

"Mm you should. And you'd be right. I am a criminal." (Literally.) I gave a tug, and he gave a moan.

"My criminal. My villain…."

"Yes," I replied at a whisper, kissing his throat. "I should be punished."

"Maybe….I will. When we have more time."

A fiendish grin spread across my face at the thought. What would a punishment entail? Would it be from Chay, or more enticing, from Falcon? The memory of Falcon over me, pinning my arms, came to my mind. The strange delight in that moment had been unexpected. Before I'd learned the truth, seeing Falcon worked up that way had a strange, intoxicating effect.

"I think I'd like that." I bit at his throat and he moaned louder. It went straight between my legs, and my hips twitched with the need to be touched again. "Touch me." My voice was a whimper.

"Could we...try something?" He straightened his head to look at me.

"Like what?"

He pushed his pants and boxers down a little more, to his thighs, then brought a hand to my hip, pulling me closer. His thighs clenched together, capturing me in their warm grip, and oh, God.

"Shit," I breathed out.

"Good?" He asked, urging me a little closer by my hip.

"Mm, yeah... Good."

Chay brought his hands to my hair, pulling me in for a kiss. I moved my hips, experimentally, and the way things slipped and gave and moved, God, I was reeling again, I was gasping for breath, and he was, too.

I loved the way it felt, and it was all *him*. Chay, Chay, Chay.

I wasn't quite sure what to do with my hands, but I brought my outer one to his hip to urge him to move with me, and that earned an enthusiastic moan and some lip nibbling. I wasn't sure we were doing any of this right, but God, it felt damn good, and if that didn't mean it was right, then I wasn't sure what did.

Chay removed his outward hand from my hair, bringing it down to touch himself as we pressed against each other. We kept kissing, moaning, gasping, writhing, and then we were jolting, shuddering, trembling. I became lost in him, in this bliss and fire-hot pleasure.

And then I was coming, and he followed, and we had hot, sticky messes on our bellies and between his thighs. That part, I wasn't fond of. I pulled a face at the sensation.

But Chay. Chay... He was beautiful. All unkempt and glistening with sweat and eyes glazed and still gasping for air. So I focused on that. Kissed him again.

"Christ, was that amazing for you, too?" I asked against his lips.

"Mhm." I felt his smile against my own. "Love you, Ava. So much." He held me to him, making me aware of the stickiness again, which he didn't seem to mind.

"I love you, too. So damn much. That's why I'm not letting go."

That made him hold on tighter, tremble a little. "Good. I don't want you to."

"I won't. Never," I said, kissing his cheeks, his nose, his brow. "Never."

CHAYTON

ONCE I CAUGHT my breath and came down from the afterglow, reality set in.

I wanted to stay. I had to talk to Dy. We had to sort all this out. I wanted to fall into a void (with Ava) rather than do that. My anxiety was a raging demon in my belly.

"I guess... We should get cleaned up, huh? Kaiden probably can't keep them away forever."

"Pff. Probably not. I'd prefer not for us to look like we just sexed it up in Kaiden's bed." Ava shuddered as he said that.

Not the best place for a first time, I guessed. But at least it'd be memorable? I wouldn't ever forget Ava to begin with. But yeah. Kaiden would never shut up about this if he caught us in the middle of straightening up.

Ava scooted carefully off the bed, trying not to drip anything or touch it either. He ended up touching his stomach and grimaced.

"I'm not sure I like this part," he grumbled. I put my face in a pillow to hide my amused smile at how ridiculously cute that was.

"I'm sorry," I said.

"For what?"

"The gross part." I glanced up. Ava was walking to the far end of the room, towards a door with slick bathroom tile shining from the doorway.

He shrugged as he went through. "We can't really help it. It's uh...natural. Right?" After some rummaging and running water, Ava returned with a damp and a dry towel.

"Yeah, I know. But, um..." My face burned as I took the offered towels. "Maybe we could use condoms. Next time." If there was a next time. I hoped he wanted a next time. But no matter what he wanted, he wanted this, he wanted *us*, and so did I. Anything was wonderful.

Ava spluttered a little before replying. "Yeah. Okay." He was red to his neck. I smiled wide again, it was so dang cute. I loved this side of him. It was a side only I got to see. The fumbling, sweet, bad at words Ava.

I loved it, along with all the other moods, even the dark, broody, grumpy one I'd first met.

My mind wandered back to Dy's words as we finished

cleaning up, about how I'd been drawn to Ava, how there was *something* about him. When we'd first met, I'd found him captivating, magnetizing, though I hadn't known why. Something about him just sucked me in. I could spot him in a crowd without even looking for him. He had this menacing presence like no one else.

Because he was a Fallen.

So how much of it was him and how much was actually my own feelings?

Maybe, when I'd first been drawn to him, that was the reason. But then, as I got to know him, I started to see him. The way he never put up a facade like other people, his bluntness, and underneath all the cynicism, a wick of humor (even if it was on the sardonic side). All these things were what made up Ava, what made him unique, and what made me fall for him in the first place. Not the fact that he was part fallen angel.

Ava was one-of-a-kind. He was special, and amazing, and caring (once I got through the prickly outer layer).

What Dy said hadn't been true. If I didn't have to let go of him, I wouldn't. I wanted to do whatever it took to hold onto him.

CHAPTER NINETEEN

CHAYTON

THERE WAS A knock on the door. Our time was up.

"Chay, wait—" Ava grabbed onto my arm as I was getting up.

"It'll be okay, Ava. We can talk things through with Dy."

Ava pulled a face at that, but his hand relaxed. We moved to the door, side by side. His hand found mine as his other went to the door handle, and I squeezed his hand tightly. Even as my anxiety threatened to swallow me and my self doubt screamed at me, Ava's fingers laced with mine were a comfort. Whatever happened, we'd face it together.

Ava opened the door, and the first thing that greeted us was Kaiden with a sheepish grin on his face. Dy stood tall behind him, a hand on the back of Kaiden's neck.

"Sorry, guys. I stalled them as long as I could."

Ava sighed beside me, but I was unsurprised. This made it easier for us to get this over with, anyways.

"Come on, Chay. Let's go."

When Dy looked so stern, so full of authority like this, saying no was the hardest thing. After all, he was a father figure to me. But I remembered my own words to Ava: *When you love someone, you don't let go.*

I wouldn't. Not without a fight. And even then.

With a breath to steady myself and another squeeze of Ava's hand to bolster my confidence, I said the word. "No."

Dy had already started turning away from us. He went ridgid, turning his head slowly back to me with a look of disbelief.

"What did you say?"

Another squeeze of Ava's hand. *I'm here,* it said. His hand was warmer than it had been a second ago, and I had to wonder if that was intentional, an additional layer of comfort.

"I...said no. We need to talk about all this."

"What else is there to talk about, Chay?" Dy put his hand on my shoulder, making me tense where it'd once brought me comfort. "He's *dangerous.*"

"*He's* right here, you know," Ava snapped. "And I'm not the monster you've made me out to be."

"You don't deny you're dangerous, then?" Dy's grip on my shoulder tightened, almost painfully.

Ava scoffed in reply, and Dy shoved Kaiden away to take my other arm, trying to pull me away from Ava.

"Hey!" Kaiden whined. Tah helped him up and held onto him, immediately clapping a hand over his mouth to keep him quiet. I appreciated the gesture. Unlike Ona, Kaiden was incapable of not butting in with his personal commentary.

"Stop, Dy!" I tightened my hand around Ava's and pulled away from his grasp. Ava caught me with his other arm, hand on my shoulder. I had to resist the urge to turn and bury myself against him and wish to fade away. I had to face this all head on. Or there would be no more him and me. "He's not going to turn into one of those demons!" My voice cracked more than I'd liked.

"How do we know he's not lying?" Dy asked. "He's of the same ilk as the demons. We can't trust him, Chay. Even if he gives his word. How do we know something won't change?"

"*I* trust him. Dy, I love him." I allowed myself to inch a little closer to Ava. His hand ran down my shoulder and arm. I took in the sensation, remembered moments ago how close together we'd been and the intimacy and that Ava had trusted *me* with that. And I would trust him with everything, too. "I can't just let go of that. Please, just give him a chance to prove that he's not dangerous and won't turn into a monster."

"And what about his little stint as Raven? I *know* what he's capable of, Chay."

"That's behind him, now. Right, Ava?" I met his eyes, took in his turned down lips and fierce glare directed at Dy. To my relief, he nodded. "See? He's not going to be a problem." My eyes shifted between Dy and Ava, neither of them moving, both staring so hard at each other I half expected Ava to combust and Dy to blow it out with his wind.

"I still don't trust him" Dy said, not taking his eyes off Ava.

Ava shifted on his feet. "I'm not going to hurt anyone. And I'm not going to turn into a monster. I'd have to intentionally devour human souls to turn into a demon, and no way am I doing that," he said.

"Who's that?" Ona said.

Ava's eyes went wide. I turned my head at the same time as Dy turned around. A winged figure landed. I'd only seen him once, but I recognized him immediately. After all, he had the same eyes as Ava, the same set to his jaw.

Makani.

"Who are you?" Dy asked.

Makani looked between all of us, brows pinched together.

"Dad, what're you doing here?" Ava stepped forward, around Dy, keeping his hold on my hand. Dy gave me a confused glance as I moved past him with Ava.

"There was a large disruption in this area. Avari, what happened? Who are all these people?"

"Um. Friends of Chayton's. It's complicated."

"You're his father?"

Makani looked to Dy. "Yes. I'm Makani."

None of us had our wings out right now, otherwise I expected he might be more confused. He'd seen me with mine before, but Ava hadn't really explained anything then.

"Look, Dyami. I'm not going to turn into a demon. My dad's not and he's been fighting against the demons for hundreds of years. See? Explain to them, Dad." Ava gestured towards his dad.

"Whoa, you're his dad?" Ona chimed in, stepping closer without a second thought. Dy and Tah stayed in place, Dy glaring, and Tah holding Kaiden, who was trying to talk, but it only came out as muffled hums. "Why don't we all talk this out, huh, Dy?" Ona turned back towards Dy. "I bet Avari's dad could tell us a lot, and address some of our concerns. Right?" Ona looked to Makani again.

"I know not what has transpired here, but shall certainly try my best to address your concerns about

Avari." Makani shot a look towards Ava that made him straighten up. "Among my own that have brought me here."

"See? Let's go inside and talk. What do you say, Dy?" Ona put a hand on Dy's shoulder.

All eyes were on Dy now. Some of the tension fell from his shoulders as he exhaled.

Dy nodded. "Fine."

The anxiety in my gut was already uncoiling at Dy's agreement. We filed into Kaiden's door; Dy, followed by Tah and Kaiden, whose mouth was now uncovered and had started rambling on, "Oh, my God! This is some juicy stuff! What a bunch we are, huh? And here I am, the only one without wings. Talk about the odd one out!" Tah kept shushing him but it wasn't helping. Ona was ahead of Ava and I, all sunshine and rainbows and "let's all get along," and behind us, Ava's dad.

Kaiden plopped onto his couch without a care in the world. Ona happily took a seat there as well. "Hi there," Ona said to Kaiden, with a bright, innocent smile. "If it isn't loud distraction guy."

"That's me!" Kaiden grinned with pride. Tah came to stand behind the couch, halfway between Ona and Kaiden, eyes on Kaiden as if poised to shut him up again on command.

Dy stayed standing, as did Makani, both pillars of strength in different ways. One to me, the other to Ava. Two father figures. Two strong people. I shuddered at the thought of who would win in a battle between the two.

I wasn't sure whether Ava and I should sit or stand. Ava was ridgid, probably not too keen to move closer to Dy; we only ended up taking a couple steps inside towards Makani.

Once we were all inside, Makani turned to Ava. "Avari. I thought I made myself perfectly clear that you were not to attract any more demons."

"I know —I—I'm sorry."

"Oh my God, this is like a big urban fantasy soap opera!" Kaiden commented in the background.

Tah stifled him with his hand again and mumbled, "Will you shut up, man?"

"I don't want to see any harm to you because you were reckless. Attracting the demons to you only makes it harder for me to protect you and Chayton. If anything were to happen to you, I wouldn't be able to use divine healing on you as I did Chayton before."

Ava squeezed my hand at the mention of my demon encounter. Dy's eyes went wide.

"You...What? You were injured by a demon, Chay?" Dy stepped towards me, putting his hands on my shoulders as if to check me for wounds.

"Dy, it's okay now. I'm fine. It was a couple months ago. I...went after Ava, and some demons were there..." I looked to the floor, biting at my lip, biting back the memory even as I tried to recall it. My hand came to my chest, right over the phantom scar. "One of them stabbed me. And if it weren't for Makani, I wouldn't have survived."

Dy still looked concerned, but turned to Makani. "You're a Fallen...and you saved Chay?"

"That is correct," Makani said with a nod. "I fight the demons, as I have for thousands of years."

"And you're still...you." Dy took a step closer to him.

"I am."

"I didn't think it was possible." Dy shook his head. "We were told all the Fallen had turned to demons."

"By whom?" Makani asked.

"Our ancestors."

"That does not surprise me. I may be the only one left

You fight the demons?" Makani had a hand to his chin now, eyes on Dy and full of keen interest. "You possess abilities such as Chayton?"

"We do. Usually we stay in the northern midwest."

"Interesting. I thought the humans bestowed with angelic gifts were no more. It was surprising to find one with Avari, but to find there are actually four still living..."

"You knew about this, Dad?"

"Yes. It was long ago, when there were still a few Fallen. A regimen of Angels came to Earth to help cull the demons. I heard an Angel called Azrael offered a group of humans the power of Angels in order to help fight the demons."

"That's right. Azrael was his name." Dy said. He turned to me again. "Chay."

"Yeah?" My heart jumped into my throat and my voice nearly croaked. The look on his face was still serious, but unreadable.

"I'm sorry. I was wrong."

"What?" Surely, I was hearing things.

"I didn't realize a Fallen could be kind and caring, or fight back against the demons. But Makani is proof of that. And he knows the name of the Angel who passed the gifts to our ancestors."

"And Ava?"

Dy eyed him, then nodded. "He obviously cares about you."

"Damn right I do."

"Then I have one thing to ask. Stay out of trouble. If you can do that, then I'll leave you two be."

"Deal," Ava said without hesitation.

"And I can stay here? With Ava?" I asked, still plagued with uncertainty at what I was hearing.

"Yes. You can stay."

And just like that, it was over. The nervous lump in my throat loosened, and my nerves eased. It was like the sun coming out.

CHAPTER TWENTY

AVARI

"WE SHOULD HEAD out," Dyami said. "Ona, Tah." Dyami waved a hand, and both of them started towards the door with him, Ona with a cheerful "All right!" and Tah begrudgingly removing his hand from Kaiden, who immediately started blabbing again. Oh, how I hadn't missed that.

"Should we go, too?" Chay asked me, tightening his hold on my hand, looking at me with the first hint of hopefulness and light I'd seen from him since Dyami showed up.

"Sure." I waved a hand at Kaiden without looking at him. "Later."

"Whaaat? You're just gonna drop all these truths and crap on me and leave me?! Dude! Can't the hot one at least stay?"

"I'm tired, man," I said. All I wanted was a nice, long nap with Chay in my arms. I wanted to be alone for the rest of what little spring break we had left. I hadn't been keeping track.

"You're dishing to me later, then! I saw those bed sheets were rumpled, mister!" Kaiden hollered as we were walking to the door. I hurried the rest of the way out, face burning. God damn it, Kaiden. Of course he noticed. Great.

As we stepped outside, my dad caught my shoulder. "Could we go for a fly? I'd like to talk to you a while more. In private."

"Uh." I glanced at Chay.

"I'll be fine. Go on. I'll meet you back at your room." Chay offered me a smile, which didn't comfort me much. But it was a real smile, and that shot straight through to my heart.

"All right." I gave his hand one last squeeze before turning to leave with my dad.

"Makani," Dyami said. My dad glanced back at him. "We will help cull the demons here, as long as we need to."

"I appreciate the assistance. Thank you." He gave a nod to Dyami, then took off.

He was quiet the whole way, flying ahead of me. I followed silently, stomach churning. Something about his hard stare as we took to the air unsettled my nerves.

We landed atop the Golden Gate, and even though this place was normally calming to me, it did nothing to soothe me at the moment. There were as many bad memories as good ones here for me, all of which seemed like ages ago.

"Avari, I'm disappointed in you. Do you realize the damage you've done? How many demons are now swarming this area?"

"I'm sorry, Dad. It's just—I didn't want to lose Chay. I almost lost him once before."

"Sometimes we have to make those sacrifices to protect those we love, son. I thought I made that clear before. I wanted you to be able to live peacefully, without the burdens I've had to endure. Without having to leave someone you loved, as I had to with Arya. Now I wonder if I should have let you stay."

"Dad, no! Don't say that!" My heart clenched at his words, at the thought of having to leave Chay for good this time, and no amount of words or actions would convince my father otherwise.

"What else am I supposed to think? You continue to draw attention, you attract swarms of demons. You are young, and naive, and you might meet your end if you do not learn to restrain yourself!"

His voice came harshly, all fiery heat that hit my chest like a brand, made my stomach drop and my conscience stab.

I wasn't used to being yelled at. Plenty of times I'd been yelled about. That kid has the demon in him, that boy isn't right, get him out of my house, yada yada yada. This was different. This was gut wrenching and guilt inducing and I'd never felt so small, so much like a child, as right now, as for the first time in my life I was being chided by my parent.

"Avari?" His voice was lighter now, concerned. When I looked up he reached out and touched my cheek, brushing away my sudden tears. Why was I crying?

"Ah, shit—I-I'm sorry," I mumbled and turned my face away, wiping my eyes.

I hated crying, it was so goddamn embarrassing.

"Shh, it is all right. It's okay." His arms came around me, held me close. "Shh."

"I'm sorry, I'm sorry," I repeated. It'd never feel like enough. I'd let him down and God was this what it felt like, to have a family? To have someone care about you?

"You still have so much to learn, things I could have taught you if only I had been there. If only I had known about you. I should not have left you again. I see that now."

"What do you mean? Are you going to stay?"

"I think I should. We need to talk about the demons as well." He released me after giving me a pat on the back.

"What about them?"

"The amount of activity around here is...concerning. Even with you drawing them, it seems excessive."

I straightened up. That, I hadn't expected. More chiding maybe, or telling me to lie low. "What does that mean?"

"There may be other forces at work here. I fear an Archdemon may be walking on Earth."

"An Archdemon?"

"Yes. Archdemons are the demons that were once fallen angels."

"Seriously?" My skin prickled, and my blood ran cold at the thought. An actual Archdemon. What were they like? Were they less monstrous, more sentient, like people?

"So far the demons have only been after you. If their creator is here, though, they might start attacking humans." He brought a hand to my shoulder and squeezed it as he pinned me with a hard look. "Listen to me, Avari. If there is an Archdemon here, it is imperative that you stay hidden, for your protection. You mustn't fight any more demons."

"But what about you? Dad, I can help—"

"I have plenty of help now with Dyami and the other artifact wielders. And I have dealt with an Archdemon before. I can do it again, if need be."

Rage boiled inside me at the mention of Dyami. So he got

to be all buddy-buddy with my dad and fight alongside him, but his own son couldn't? Like hell. Dyami was a dick, and I still didn't like him, even though Chay was staying here. Chay could do whatever he wanted, he was a grown ass adult and could make his own decisions, and so could I.

"Please, Dad. There's got to be something I can do. I can't just stand by twiddling my thumbs while all of you fight. I can't."

He stared at me, while I glared at him as sternly as possible. His face softened, and he sighed.

"You are as stubborn as your mother, you know."

My heart clenched. "She was stubborn?"

He smiled wistfully and nodded. "When we met, she insisted I stay with her until I was fully recovered. She made certain that I got enough rest and to eat, two things I never had in abundance my whole existence. She was so caring and kind. She would have worried after you. It is only right I should take care of you in her place. I want you to be safe."

"I understand. But it sounds like you need someone to look out for you, too."

I reached out tentatively and put my hand over his, squeezing. I was so unused to this, to the idea of familial affection. But it didn't feel wrong. He put his other hand over mine and smiled.

"You are right. Would you accept a compromise?"

"Like what?" I tilted my head, mirroring him, curious.

"You have a great deal to learn. Since I plan to remain in the area, what do you say to some lessons? I can teach you everything I know, so if ever a time comes when I cannot fight and protect you, you can fight back. Until then, I do not want you going out seeking a fight without me."

"I think that's a great compromise," I said, with a smile.

"You've got yourself a deal, Dad."

He returned the smile and pulled me into a one armed hug, his hand coming to rest on the back of my head. "Very good. I love you...Son."

The warm fuzzies overcame me, pooling in my chest, clawing at my throat and making it hard to breathe or speak. I leaned into his chest, took in his warmth and strength and stability.

"I love you, too, Dad."

It seemed an impossible thing, to have my dad here, and Chay by my side. I had people I cared about. I finally felt like I had a place, like I had reasons to be selfless, in a world full of selfishness.

CHAYTON

"WE SHOULD TALK more, too, Chay. Fly with us?" Dy asked after Ava and his father left.

I nodded. The monster of anxiety in my belly had shrunk to a small, manageable thing now that the immediate fear of leaving had passed.

Dy led the way, Ona and Tah on his flanks and me not far behind them. We landed in the park nearby the marina, among some trees to obscure us.

"What did you want to talk about?"

"What happens next," Dy said. "It looks like we'll need to stay in the area awhile, to handle demons, and to train you."

A bile of uneasiness rose in my throat at the thought of training to fight the demons. They were so terrifying, I wasn't sure I'd ever be able to.

"And after that?" I asked, straining for my voice not to crack.

"That's up to you, coz. You don't have to come home with us. But if you stay, you might have to be on watch of this area by yourself."

I bit my lip as I considered that. There was Ava and Kaiden, of course. But Ava attracted demons and Kaiden had no super abilities, despite how good he was with knives. I couldn't put any of this on them. I hoped I wouldn't have to, and that once things calmed down, they stayed calm.

"It'll be okay, man. We've got your back, and once we've got everything under control, things'll probably be super boring!" Ona said, grasping my shoulder and squeezing. "Right, Dy?"

Boring. That was something I looked forward to.

"Right." Dy clasped my other shoulder. "Don't worry too much about it. For now, focus on yourself and the present. Okay?"

"Okay."

"There's one more thing," Dy said. "You can't be a public superhero anymore. Falcon, as the people know him, must disappear."

"We have to keep anonymity for our protection," Tah added.

I closed my eyes and let out a breath. "Right. I understand."

Actually, I was relieved. For a while, I'd felt like it was a burden to hold that torch.

"Your time as Falcon the superhero may be over, but your time as Falcon the protector is just beginning," Dy said. "We'll be right here by your side, as long as you need us. Okay?" Dy rubbed my arms and looked into my eyes. It grounded me, eased my panic.

Falcon, the invisible protector.

Even though the struggle against the demons would be an unseen one to the public, I wouldn't be alone in it. This new Falcon didn't have to always be there, always be strong, a pillar of justice and upstanding citizen, while secretly dating a menace to society.

"Okay."

Dy pulled me into a tight hug. "I'm sorry I derailed everything for you there for a bit, Chay. And I'm sorry I knocked you for a loop before. I didn't mean to. If you need anything, just let me know."

"Thanks, Dy."

AVARI

CHAY WAS WAITING for me outside my dorm building.

The smile he greeted me with was like a gravitational pull, dragging me down from orbit. I wanted to crash into him, like two colliding meteors, and never come apart.

I settled for a nonchalant, "Hey."

"Hey. How did things go with your dad?" he asked as I let us in and we walked to my room.

"He was a bit upset with me, but it's okay."

As soon as we were in my room, I pulled him into a tight hug, resting my head on his shoulder. He stroked my hair and kissed it. I melted in his arms. This was my heaven. This was my place. With Chay.

"No leaving. Ever again," I said.

"Okay."

We inched towards the bed. I sat down, while Chay came to kneel in front of me.

"I think I like you like this," I said, stroking his hair as a smirk came across my face.

Chay caught one of my hands and kissed my palm. "On my knees?"

"Mhm..." He started massaging my palm, running his fingers over my callouses, making me lose all train of thought. God, that was good. His touch was better than I ever could have imagined another person's being. I bit back a moan. "S-So..." I started. He looked up at me with a hint of mischievousness in his eyes and that bright, sunshine smile I so loved, and it was so damn hard not to push him to the floor instead of speaking right now. "What happens now?"

"Enjoy the rest of our spring break?" He was kissing the pads of my fingers now, and it was heavenly and sinful at the same time. The sensation was overwhelming and almost unbearable and yet, because it was Chay, my love, my light, it was so, so good.

"What little we have left? God, you're making it really hard to think right now..."

"I think...I've had enough thinking for now." He brought a hand to cup the back of my neck and pulled me in for a peck on the lips. "I want to forget everything else for now, except you and me. I want you." He laced our fingers and kissed my knuckles. "I want to be boring college boyfriends for a while."

He was beginning to sound like me. Completely and utterly selfish. For once, Chay was only thinking of himself, of us. I could get used to that.

I kissed him firmly on the lips, and when I pulled back, I was beaming at him.

"I want that, too. And...you owe me a punishment, for

being a criminally bad influence."

Chay beamed back at me. "I do," he said, then pushed me back onto the bed and proceeded to kiss me.

I held onto him, let myself get lost, let myself be selfish. Chay was my light, and I never had to let him go. Whatever else came next, we'd face it together.

About the Author

Amara Lynn has always been a quiet daydreamer. Coming up with characters and worlds since childhood, Amara eventually found an outlet in writing. Amara loves anything to do with pirates, villains and superheroes, angels and demons.

Amara is addicted to music and gets the most inspiration from moving songs and lyrics. When not writing, Amara usually reads, listens to podcasts, watches anime, plays a video game here and there (but mostly collects them), and takes way too many cat pictures.

Amara is non-binary/enby and queer and uses they/them pronouns.

For more updates on Amara's work, visit their website: https://amarajlynn.wordpress.com/

Lightning Source UK Ltd.
Milton Keynes UK
UKHW040737130921
390494UK00001B/143